WHERE THE LEOPARD
PASSES

WHERE THE LEOPARD PASSES

A BOOK OF AFRICAN FOLK TALES

by

GERALDINE ELLIOT

"Where the Leopard passes
There, also, will Kalulu go"
Old African saying

Illustrated by
SHEILA HAWKINS

With a Foreword by
LAURA SIMMS

SCHOCKEN BOOKS · NEW YORK

First published by Schocken Books 1968
First Schocken paperback edition 1987
10 9 8 7 6 5 4 3   87 88 89 90

Library of Congress Catalog No. 68–21827

Manufactured in the United States of America
ISBN   0–8052–0847–X

To
HUMPHREY
with my love

CONTENTS

FOREWORD

WHERE THE LEOPARD PASSES is a lovely collection of genuine East African folktales of the Ngoni People. They have been rewritten for children by a European woman, Geraldine Elliot. She heard them told by Ngoni grandmothers when she was a child at the turn of the century. The stories themselves are like the character Kalulu, the Rabbit. They are small, but filled with ideas, wisdom, humor, and valuable information.

The essence of these stories is authentically African. I have heard and read many variants of each of these stories. But, these retellings are very European, ornamented with colorful descriptions of animal life, villages, and landscapes and enlivened with charming dialogue. The author is like Leopard, Nyalugwe, who makes pathways through the jungle for Rabbit to follow. Through her vivid additions to the stories Geraldine Elliot provides us with visual and psychological pathways into a world very different from our own. Of course, we did not trick her, as Kalulu tricked Leopard. But perhaps she has generously tricked us into enjoying the Ngoni literature and landscape, just as she did when she was a child.

I suggest that you read these tales out loud. The language is beautiful and it is not simplified for children. It inspires questions and stretches the mind and imagination. The use of the Chinyasa or tribal names evokes a special place and time. The sounds and rhythms of the words give the book a feeling of history and authenticity. The author writes, "It seems to me only right that I should keep to the original names. They

ix

are nice names, and at least no one will be worried by 'Kalulu,' the Rabbit." For, as you will read, Kalulu would interfere if proper behavior among the creatures were forgotten. Rabbit, like all the other animals, is not just an ordinary Rabbit. He is the first Rabbit, the Ancestor. His actions have an effect in the present. For example, what happened to Tortoise in those long ago days caused all tortoises to have cracked shells, and so on.

Animal stories are teaching stories. The lessons in each tale are obvious. But as one reads them again and again, more detail and subtler meanings emerge. The fun and the poignancy of these narratives come from the personality of the animals: they are human. In hearing their stories, we learn much about ourselves and our world.

Perhaps today, the retelling of these African stories for children is more vital than when they were first published. We stand at the threshold of a time when we may lose access to the wisdom and teachings of traditional peoples and those who heard folkstories firsthand from traditional storytellers. With the prevalence of the electronic media in our lives, we may also simply forget the many benefits of reading or telling a story to our children. Folktales transmit a sense of human dignity and teach the interrelationships between all things. They assure children of a continuous history as old as time, of which they too are a part. And the very telling of the story is an intimate event that brings us together and renews our faith in human goodness and the power of communication. The gift of these stories is limitless in a child's life.

Now, the cleverness of Kalulu, the wisdom of Tortoise's wife, the strength of Leopard, the humility of Ram, the foolishness of Spider, the beauty of sapphire blue Starling, and the lovable laziness of Zebra will not be forgotten.

LAURA SIMMS

WHERE THE LEOPARD
PASSES

1

KALULU AND THE LEOPARD

BLACK and tawny as the shadow underneath the sunlit tree the Leopardess sprawled, lazily grooming herself as she chatted to the wife of Kalulu, the rabbit.

"My husband is the bravest of all the animals," she said proudly. "And by far the most handsome."

"He certainly is handsome," agreed the Rabbit's Wife, "but," she added, "my husband is the cleverest."

"Mine is clever, too," countered the Leopardess, with some asperity. She knew quite well that Nyalugwe, the Leopard, was not clever, but she was not going to make such an admission to Kalulu's Wife. "And he is so skilful," she went on. "Kalulu can't make jungle tracks like Nyalugwe! And he is strong."

"Kalulu isn't very strong," the Rabbit's Wife admitted. "Just brave, clever and handsome."

"Handsome? My dear! With those ears?" The Leopardess opened her eyes wide with surprise and looked at the Rabbit's Wife as if she could not really have meant what she said.

"*I* think so," said Kalulu's Wife defiantly.

"Well! There's no accounting for tastes! I'm afraid I don't admire long ears and plain coats myself." The Leopardess glanced carelessly at her own lovely markings as she spoke, then rose slowly to her feet, stretched and said she must be going. Nyalugwe, her husband, had been away in search of corn and she wished to be at home to welcome him on his return.

The Leopardess left, and, shortly after, Kalulu, the Rabbit, came back from a morning visit to Njobvu, the Elephant, and his wife told him of the Leopardess and all that she had said.

"Nyalugwe certainly is strong and handsome," Kalulu agreed, "and certainly he is not clever. Nor is he kind, for he likes to frighten the Smaller Animals. I wonder if he *really* is brave? I think I'll try and find out!"

A mischievous glint came into Kalulu's eye as he grinned at his wife and thoughtfully stroked a whisker. Then: "Have we any Bees-wax?" he asked.

"Yes," said his wife.

"Wax . . . a pair of horns . . . some feathers . . . and my spear. That's what I want. And you must help me to dress up."

"O-ho!" laughed Kalulu's Wife. "This promises to be fun! There are some fine Turaco feathers and you must have red earth and white clay to smear on your face and chest. We will make you look extremely fierce and frightening and then we shall see how brave Leopard really is!"

* * * * *

The sun was sinking as Nyalugwe, the Leopard, left the village grain-store and set off towards the track that led up to the rocky hillside where he lived. He was well pleased with himself, for his basket was full of corn and he had enjoyed his day and had been greatly amused at the alarm his appearance had caused in the village.

How the chickens had clucked and squawked! How the goats had bleated! One young kid, at whom he had snarled, had looked as if it would die of fright. Really very funny, it had been!

The path wound uphill and across a gully strewn with giant boulders—a dark and sunless spot where no one save a few snakes cared to live. Sound echoed queerly and there was always something sinister about the place. Unconsciously the Leopard quickened his pace and hurried round the corner of one of the great rocks. As he did so, a blood-curdling cry echoed up and down the gully. Nyalugwe's heart missed a beat and then seemed to stand quite still, for there, in front of him, stood a most fearsome figure. Its face bore hideous markings of red and white. Its head was adorned with horns and feathers and a pair of Rabbit's ears. It carried a spear and advanced on Nyalugwe with wild leaps and yells.

For a moment Leopard was so paralysed with fear that he could not think or move. Then, as the Thing was almost on him, he gave one screech, dropped his basket of corn and bounded up the rock and raced away.

The Thing sat down and laughed. It laughed until its sides ached; it laughed until the tears ran down its painted face; it laughed until it felt quite ill. Then it picked up the basket and trotted off home, chuckling all the way.

Next day, Kalulu's Wife set out to return the basket and had not gone far when she met the Leopardess.

"Oh," began the Leopardess, "such a terrible thing happened to Nyalugwe yesterday as he was coming home. He was attacked by a fearsome monster in the dark gully. Of course he fought it with the greatest bravery and drove it away, but he was quite exhausted when he got home. And naturally he lost his basket of corn in the fight. Is it not a shocking thing?" She paused. "Why, Mrs. Rabbit, surely you are not laughing?" Her

3

voice was stiff and haughty. "It is no laughing matter, I can assure you!"

"Oh, but it is!" wailed the Rabbit's Wife. "It is very funny indeed! You see, it wasn't a fearsome monster that Nyalugwe met in the dark gully. It was Kalulu, who had dressed up for fun. See, here is your basket. Kalulu told me how scared Nyalugwe was and how he had dropped it in his fright and had run away. My, how it made Kalulu laugh!"

"Oh! For shame! And Nyalugwe never ran away!" The Leopardess was trembling with indignation. "How dare Kalulu dress up and frighten Nyalugwe. It's disgraceful, absolutely disgraceful! And how dare he laugh! And you, too! I shall go and tell Nyalugwe about this at once."

Swish went an angry tail and every whisker bristled with rage, as the Leopardess turned and hastened home. And when Nyalugwe heard her story, he foamed at the mouth, he lashed his tail to and fro, he stamped up and down, stopping every now and then to sharpen his claws against the trunk of a tree and anyone could see that he was wishing that the tree was Kalulu, the Rabbit. Nyalugwe was furious!

"Just let me get hold of that Rabbit!" he snarled. "I'll thrash him for this. The insolence of the creature! He thought it funny, did he? He laughed, did he? Laughed! At me, Nyalugwe! Oh, I'll give him a thrashing he'll never forget. I'll teach him a lesson!"

Now it happened that a Bee was passing as Nyalugwe uttered these threats and, since the Bee was a friend of Kalulu's, he flew straight off to warn the Rabbit of the Leopard's intentions. Kalulu was very grateful and, just in case Leopard did mean what he said, Rabbit at once made plans to outwit him. First of all he arranged for a trap to be dug on the path that led to his home and then he paid a hurried call on his friends Njati, the Buffalo, and Njobvu, the Elephant, to ask if they would give him

4

their help. This they were delighted to do, especially when Kalulu promised them each a honey-comb, and they listened carefully to the Rabbit's instructions and then proceeded to carry them out while Kalulu went off, smiling cheerfully, to look for a long, strong rope of wild vine.

* * * * *

"I'll thrash that Rabbit until he'll wish he had never been born. I'll teach him to laugh at me!"

Nyalugwe's fury had, if anything, increased as he recalled the scene in the dark gully and remembered how scared he had been. All the way down the hillside he brooded on his wounded dignity, and he was so busy thinking how insulted he felt that it was some time before he became aware of a queer moaning sound as someone in pain. Then suddenly he saw Njati, the Buffalo, limping pitifully, his leg and shoulder swathed in bandages made of banana leaves.

"Oh," groaned Njati, "I think my leg is broken. I think I am going to die. Who would have believed that Kalulu was so fierce and strong!"

"What has that insufferable Rabbit to do with it? How did you come to break your leg?" demanded Nyalugwe, without even so much as saying "I'm sorry you have been hurt."

"I had a quarrel with Kalulu and I considered that he deserved to be thrashed. But he was stronger than I and he beat me and drove me away. And here I am, bruised and broken, and I think I am going to die."

"Nonsense!" said the Leopard. "You'll be all right. And you will be glad to know that I am now on my way to give that Rabbit the thrashing of his life. I, too, have a quarrel with him."

"I hope you succeed in beating him. Oh, I do hope so! But don't underestimate his strength, as I did." Njati began to moan again and Nyalugwe continued on his way. As he stalked along he told himself that *he'd* deal

5

with that insufferable Rabbit. There would be no non-sense, as in Njati's case—though that really was very queer—anyone would have thought that Njati was far too strong to be beaten and driven away by Kalulu. But, of course, Njati was stupid and must have made

6

some foolish blunder. He, Nyalugwe, would not blunder. No fear of that!

It was at that moment that Leopard saw Njobvu, the Elephant. He was sitting forlornly by the track and weeping bitterly.

"I wouldn't have believed it!" sobbed the Elephant. "You'd think I was strong enough to beat that hateful

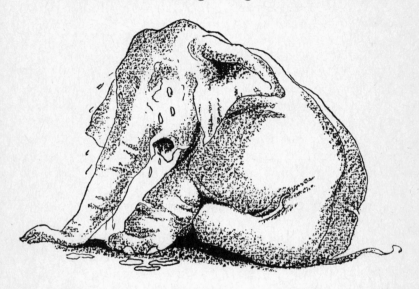

Rabbit. But, no! *He* has beaten *me*. It feels as if he has broken every bone in my poor body. I think I am going to die!"

"Nonsense," said Nyalugwe. "You don't look very bad to me. But do you mean to tell me that Kalulu has beaten you, too?"

"Yes," wailed Njobvu. "I had no idea he was so strong."

"Nor had I." Nyalugwe sounded thoughtful. Then: "Never mind," he said. "I shall succeed where you and Njati have failed and I'll thrash that Rabbit within an inch of his life."

"Oh, I do hope so," sobbed the Elephant. "That's what he needs. I do hope you'll succeed."

Nyalugwe stalked on, bristling with anger and exalted by resolve. But somewhere, deep down inside him, he felt a little wriggle, the first little wriggle of that sick, frightened feeling, and he found himself hoping that he *was* stronger that Njati and Njobvu, who were so much bigger than himself; that he *was* stronger than Kalulu, who was so much smaller than any of them but who possessed such amazing strength; that he was not being foolish . . . making a blunder . . . going to get hurt. . . .

"Ow! Help! Help!" screeched Leopard, as the ground suddenly gave way beneath him and he felt himself falling, falling, falling into the pit that Kalula had had dug and had covered over with leaves and withered grass, the pit that was a trap to catch the Leopard. For no sooner had Nyalugwe fallen in than Kalulu, who had been waiting nearby, skipped from his hiding-place and threw a noose of vine rope over the Leopard's head.

"So," said Kalulu, "I have caught you, Nyalugwe. You came to thrash me, I am told? And for what reason, I should like to know. Because you were scared when you met me in the dark gully? Because I laughed at your fright? Have you not laughed," Kalulu continued sternly, "when goats and chickens run away from you? Does it not amuse you to strike terror into the hearts of Smaller Animals? Is it not *you* who should be thrashed?"

"No, no!" shrieked Nyalugwe, his voice shrill with fear. "Don't hurt me. Set me free. Set me free, Kalulu, and I will be your friend. I will work for you if only you will set me free and will not beat me."

"Work for me? What can you do for me that I cannot do for myself?"

What indeed, wondered Nyalugwe. And yet, surely there must be something. He racked his brains.

"Ah," he exclaimed, "you cannot clear paths through the jungle as I can. I will make tracks for you, through the jungle, through the bush—wherever you wish to go. I will clear the way and you shall follow after me in comfort and in ease. If I promise to do this, will you set me free?"

Kalulu considered the matter. "H'm," he said at length. "That certainly would be pleasant. And I do not wish to be hard on you. Yes, I will agree to that, and henceforth it will be said that 'Where the Leopard passes, there also will Kalulu go'. I like the idea. Yes, I will set you free."

2

THE BABBLING REED WARBLER

I'M lucky to be alive!" said the Francolin importantly.
"Very lucky indeed. If I hadn't been able to run
so fast and if the grass hadn't been so thick, that
Hunter would have had me as sure as ants are ants. As
it is, his arrow has taken a feather out of my wing."

The Francolin was very upset, and no wonder, for she
had just been through a most alarming experience. And
it was not as if it was the first time that she had had a
narrow escape, though never before had she lost a
feather. But Nkhanga, the Guineafowl, had, and so had
the Quail, and on more than one occasion Snipe had
had to jink very quickly to dodge the Hunter's arrow.

"Is there nothing we can do to protect ourselves?" they asked each other, but they could find no answer.

"Cheer up! Cheer up! Don't look so glum!" babbled the little Reed Warbler as he ran down the stem of a flowering rush that grew beside the water-hole. "No one should look glum. I never do!"

"I don't like anyone to look glum or to be sad and unhappy," sang the Sunbird as he darted busily from flower to flower in search of nectar. "No one should be unhappy on a day like this, when the sun is shining brightly and all the flowers are beautiful and gay."

"You wouldn't be so cheerful if you had our trouble," began the Snipe.

"We all have our troubles," the Reed Warbler interrupted, "but some of us don't make such a fuss about them. I think Sunbird is quite right and I think flowers are very beautiful, so bright and gay and colourful." He babbled on, as he always did, but no one paid much attention. They all knew that the little Reed Warbler's chatter never ceased.

"You know," said Sunbird suddenly, "I think it is a pity that we birds are not coloured like the flowers. It is rather dull to be just white—all of us plain white. It would be much more fun if I were blue and you were green and Francolin were red."

"I should like to be red. No, purple. Or perhaps yellow. I wonder which would suit me best? It would be difficult to decide. Perhaps a mixture of colours . . . all the colours of the rainbow . . . ." The little Reed Warbler was off again.

"If we were green, or perhaps a dusty, browny colour, like the withered grass, we would find it easier to hide from our enemies." Snipe spoke slowly, as if he was thinking aloud. "Then, if we were to lie quite still, it would be far more difficult for them to see us."

"Yes, yes!" agreed Francolin and Quail excitedly.

"They would never see us if we were coloured like the grass instead of being white."

"I like being white," began the Egret.

"Oh, no! Colours would be much nicer!" Several birds spoke at once and dozens more arrived and asked what all the chattering was about, then they, too, began to argue and to make suggestions. At length the babble became so great that Nkhwasi, the Fish Eagle, heard it and decided to leave his fishing grounds and find out what it meant. As he landed on the thorn tree by the water-hole and folded his great wings, the chattering ceased for a moment. Then the little Reed Warbler's voice could be heard again.

"Look! There is Fish Eagle," he was saying. "I wonder what colour Nkhwasi thinks would suit me best. Shall I go and ask him?"

"No. And do stop babbling so much," said Snipe, who was getting very tired of Reed Warbler's incessant chatter.

It was Sunbird who flew up to the Fish Eagle and explained his great idea that all the birds should be coloured like the flowers and asked how this could be achieved.

Nkhwasi looked thoughtful and very, very wise. "It is a good idea," he said at length, "and if all the birds are agreed, I will fly to Mlungu, the Great Spirit, and ask if he will give us colours and make us as beautiful as the flowers. Is that what you want? Are you all agreed?"

"Yes, yes!" shrilled the Reed Warbler. "That is just what we want. And please ask if I can be the first to be coloured and say I want to be red and purple and . . ." His noisy little voice was drowned by the cries of the other birds all shouting, "Yes, yes! We want to have colours like the flowers. Yes, we are all agreed."

"I like being white," murmured Egret wistfully, but he spoke so quietly that nobody heard what he said.

"Very well," said the Fish Eagle. "I will go to Mlungu,"

and, spreading his great white wings, he flew straight up towards the sun.

*   *   *   *   *

"Me next! Me next! Do me next!" chirped the little Reed Warbler. "Do me next!"

Mlungu, who had agreed to the petition, sat on a throne surrounded by great pots of coloured dyes, while all the birds stood patiently around, waiting for their turn to be transformed. Only the Reed Warbler was impatient and kept hopping up and down and crying, "My turn next! Me next! Do me now!"

Because it had been his idea, Sunbird had been the first to be painted and had become a living jewel, flashing now green, now red, now blue, as he darted to and fro. His head, neck, throat and back gleamed with a lovely shimmering metallic green; his tail was black, the outer feathers tipped with white while the coverts held a hint of blue. His breast was scarlet, as bright and gay as any flower, and as he flew around the birds all marvelled at his beauty and the Reed Warbler chirped and chattered: "I want to be like Sunbird! I want to be all the colours of the rainbow! I want to be painted next!"

But Mlungu was painting the Oriole in shades of gold and yellow and, when Oriole was done, he painted a Green Pigeon and then he gave the Lowrie his coat of blue and green with lovely crimson wings.

"Me next! Me next! Do me now!" babbled the Reed Warbler as each bird was finished and he hopped up and down in the most irritating way. But Mlungu took no notice. Calm and serene, he beckoned to the Francolin and when she shyly asked if she and Snipe and Quail might be given colours that would help to hide them from their enemies, Mlungu smiled kindly and painted them in shades of brown and buff and grey and made them speckled and mottled, so that they looked like the sunshine and the shadows in the long grass. And to the

13

Francolin He gave red legs, salmon-coloured to the Harlequin Quail, and to the Snipe He gave legs of slaty blue.

"Me next! Me next!" chirped the Reed Warbler and impatiently hopped right on to the edge of one of the great pots of dye that stood all round the throne.

Mlungu frowned a little, then: "You shall have your wish," He said, and quickly painted the little Warbler and bade him fly away. Then He beckoned to the Egret. "You are a very beautiful white bird," He said. "Do you really wish to be changed?"

"No," said the Egret. "I am proud of my whiteness. I like being white and have no wish to be coloured like the other birds. Please let me stay as I am."

"So you shall," said Mlungu, and called the Roller to Him.

"Look at me! Look at me!" sang the Reed Warbler. "I'm more beautiful than Sunbird. I'm more beautiful than Oriole. I'm more beautiful than Lowrie. Look at me! Look at me!"

"Oh, be quiet," said the other birds and craned their necks to watch the transformation of the Roller. The pale mauve of an iris coloured his breast; his wings and tail feathers suddenly shone blue, blue as the midnight sky when the moon is full. His head took on a rich, warm, coppery brown. Lightly his head and wings were touched with emerald green, his beak was painted black, his legs an olive shade. Mlungu smiled as He added the last finishing touch and from the birds a deep sigh went up: "Oh! Oh, how beautiful!"

"I'm as beautiful as Roller," chirped the little Warbler, and ran up and down to show himself off. "Look at me' I'm just as beautiful as Roller. Am I not?" he added, as a sudden doubt assailed him. "What colours am I?" he asked. "Blue? Green? Red?"

"No," answered Snipe shortly.

"Well, what am I?"

14

"Just brown. Plain brown."

"What?" he shrieked. "Not coloured? Not like the rainbow? Not even red or purple?" The Warbler couldn't believe that he was just plain brown.

"Hush!" said Mlungu. "You chatter too much. I would have given you all the colours you wished, but you were too impatient. Try and learn to be patient, little Warbler."

Ashamed, the little Warbler hung his head while Mlungu took a humble Starling in His hand and painted him a glowing sapphire blue.

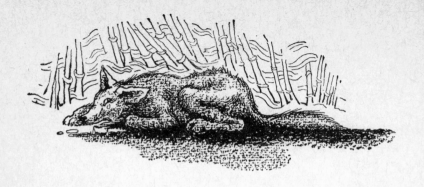

3

THE CLEVER LITTLE JACKAL

"I DON'T believe it! There *was* some honey. I know there was!"

One by one the Elephant's Wife examined the store pots with her trunk, but there was no doubt about it—the pots that should have contained honey were empty, quite, quite empty. "H'm," she thought, "that lazy, good-for-nothing husband of mine has been helping himself again. Very well, then! He can cancel that little visit he was going to pay to one of his friends this afternoon and, instead, he can go for a nice long walk in search of honey."

"Njobvu," she called. "Wake up, Njobvu! I want you to go and get some honey. We don't seem to have any left."

"What was that you said, my love?" asked the Elephant sleepily.

"There seems to be no honey left," replied the Elephant's Wife in her sweetest voice. "I thought we had plenty. It is very odd the way it has vanished." She sighed, a long, deep, tired sigh—the kind of sigh all

housewives give when they find that Someone has been at the honey.

Njobvu, the Elephant, shot a quick look at his wife. Did she suspect him, he wondered? It was hard to tell from that innocent expression she was wearing. How foolish he had been to eat it all—he ought to have left some, then she might not have noticed. But the honey had been so good, oh, so good. . . .

"I suppose we do eat rather a lot," he began.

"*We*, dear?" said his wife.

"Hurrumph!" The Elephant coughed. He didn't quite like the tone of voice in which she had said that.

"We'll have to see about getting some more."

"*We*, dear?" said his wife again.

No, thought Njobvu, he didn't like that tone of voice at all. There was no doubt about it, she *did* suspect. A pity! Perhaps he had better offer to go and fetch more honey before she got unpleasant about it.

"I think I might manage a call on the Bees to-morrow afternoon. It is a long, hot walk, but . . ."

"A long, hot walk will do you good, dear," said the Elephant's Wife firmly. "A long, hot walk *this* afternoon. Not to-morrow."

"I'm busy this afternoon," Njobvu protested. "I'm going to see . . ."

"The Bees." She finished his sentence for him. "Quite so, dear. You are going to see the Bees and persuade them to let us have a nice big bag of honey."

There was now a steely quality in the voice of the Elephant's Wife. Njobvu knew that tone only too well and he knew that he would have to go. That very afternoon. All that way, that long, hot way through the tall grass in the valley, through the thick dark jungle near the foot-hills and up the mountain-side to where the Bees had their hives in a great cleft of the rock. What a long way it was! Njobvu almost wished that he had not eaten the honey. Oh, but it had been good! He licked his lips in a reminiscent sort of way. Yes, it had been worth while. And the sooner he saw the Bees, the sooner there would be more honey for him to eat when he found himself feeling a little hungry in the morning, as he so often did. Njobvu began to feel quite cheerful again.

"Very well, my love," he said. "Just as you say, my love. I will go this afternoon."

*   *   *   *   *

At the bottom of the mountain, just where the foot-hills merged into the thick dark jungle, there lived a family of jackals—Father Jackal, Mother Jackal and three young Jackals.

Now the youngest little Jackal, who was called Nkhandwe after his father, was a very cunning little Jackal and also a very greedy little Jackal. There was hardly anything he would not eat and, most of all, he liked to eat fruit and honey. Of the two he preferred honey, perhaps because it was more difficult to get; but he liked its rich golden colour and he loved its sweet sticky taste. And it was just as he was sitting all by himself at the edge of the jungle, thinking what a fine thing it would be if only figs would grow on bushes, close to the ground so that he could reach them with ease; or if honey-combs could be found as readily as the Chitesi bean, which grew almost everywhere and was wanted by no one, when he saw Njobvu, the Elephant, coming down the mountain and, on his head, Njobvu was carrying a large bag made of plaited reeds.

What, wondered the little Jackal instantly, was in that bag? Surely it must be something to eat? What could it be? Fruit, perhaps? Perhaps honey? If only he could find out!

The little Jackal crouched down and laid his head upon his forepaws and thought and thought and thought, and all the time he never took his eyes off the Elephant who was coming closer and closer to where he lay. Suddenly a smile lit up his cunning little face. The next moment he began to cry. Tears poured down his furry pointed nose and the air was filled with bitter sobs.

"Goodness, gracious, what is all this?" exclaimed Njobvu, and hurried in the direction of the cries. "Why, whatever is the matter?" he asked, as soon as he saw the weeping Jackal.

"Boo-hoo-hoo!" sobbed little Nkhandwe. "I am so miserable. My father and my mother are dead and I am all alone in the world. There is no one to care for me. Boo-hoo-hoo!"

"You poor little Jackal!" Elephant began, with real concern and sympathy.

"My father was so wonderful," the little Jackal continued. "He was so good to me, so kind. He always used to let me ride on his back. Now there is no one to give me rides. Boo-hoo-hoo!" The little Jackal's sobs grew louder than before.

"Would you like a ride on my back?" asked Njobvu kindly.

"I c-could never g-get up there," sobbed the little Jackal.

"That's quite easy," said Elephant. "I pick you up with my trunk, like this, and up you go!" And he curled his trunk round the little Jackal, lifted him high in the air, and set him down on the top of his head, alongside the bag of honey.

"Ooh! My father couldn't have done that!" Little Nkhandwe sounded surprised and quite a lot happier.

"No, I don't suppose he could. And he couldn't squirt water out of his trunk like I can. A trunk is a very useful thing." Njobvu liked to boast about his trunk and proceeded to tell the little Jackal all the things he could do with it. And the little Jackal pretended to listen and sometimes he said, "Can you really?" and sometimes he said, "Oh, how clever!" and sometimes he said, "Fancy that!" But he wasn't *really* listening: he was scratching a hole in one corner of the bag of plaited reeds. And as he scratched, he sniffed, and grew more certain every moment that it was honey that he could smell. So he scratched faster and faster, until he had scratched right through the corner of the bag and right through the

banana leaves in which the honey-combs were wrapped.
Then the honey began to trickle out and Nkhandwe
licked it up as fast as he could, but after a time a few
drops escaped and trickled down on to the Elephant's
trunk.

"Dear me," said Njobvu, the Elephant, "is that rain
that I feel? Is it raining, little Jackal, and are you getting
wet?"

"N-no," sobbed the Jackal. "It isn't raining, Njobvu.
Perhaps they are my tears that you can feel. I am so
unhappy that I cannot stop crying. I do not think I shall
ever be happy again!" The little Jackal sobbed twice,
licked up some more honey and sobbed once more.

"You must try and be brave, little Jackal."

"I am trying, Njobvu. But I can't help remembering
all the kind things my father used to do and how he
used to find such lovely fig trees and how he used to let
me stand on his neck and pick the figs. I suppose you
couldn't find a fig tree?"

"Why, yes, there is a fig tree not far from here," replied
Njobvu. "I noticed it as I came by. Shall I take you
there?"

"That would be k-kind," sobbed the Jackal. "I think
I should feel happier if I c-could see a fig tree once
again." This time the little Jackal was speaking the
truth, for the honey was nearly finished and he dearly
loved to eat figs.

"Very well," said the Elephant, and hurried on until
he came to the tree that he had noticed earlier in the day.
It was a fine tree, thickly covered with leaves and laden
with ripe figs and its branches almost touched the
ground. Just the sort of tree, in fact, that Nkhandwe
hoped it would be.

"Oh," he said, with one last sob, "thank you, Njobvu.
This is indeed a fine tree. It is almost as fine as the trees
my father used to find." With that, he crammed his
mouth full of figs, swung himself into the tree and, under

cover of the thick leaves, scuttled quickly to the ground and scampered away as fast as he could.

"Are you enjoying yourself?" asked Elephant after a while.

There was no answer.

"Little Jackal, where are you?"

Still no answer.

"Little Jackal, I can't stay here all day. I still have a long walk home and soon it will be getting dark. Do you not want me to carry you any further?"

Not a sound. Not even a rustle in the underbush.

"Well," thought Njobvu, "what a queer way to behave! But I really can't stay here any longer. I hope nothing has happened to the little Jackal. Perhaps I had better call once more." Njobvu made a loud trumpeting noise and called again: "Nkhandwe! Jackal! I'm going home!"

The sound came faintly to the little Jackal as he raced along and he laughed a little as he ran. Honey, figs, and a ride on the Elephant's back, all in one afternoon! My, but he'd been clever! What a tale to tell the family when he got back!

Njobvu, the Elephant, looked very puzzled as he resumed his long walk home.

* * * * *

"Well, dear," said the Elephant's Wife, "I hope you have had a nice long walk, and have brought back plenty of honey? You've been gone a long time, I must say. But I've had visitors while you have been away. Who do you think? Nkhandwe, the Jackal, and his wife, Mkasi."

Njobvu, the Elephant, was removing the bag of honey from his head and he was just thinking that it seemed very light when the meaning of his wife's words began to penetrate. He stared at her amazed. "Who did you say?" he demanded, his voice hoarse with suspicion.

"Did you say Nkhandwe, the Jackal, and his wife, Mkasi?"

"Yes, dear, They could talk of nothing but their youngest son. Such a clever little Jackal, they tell me. . . . Why, whatever is the matter, Njobvu?" The Elephant's wife had never seen such a look of fury on

her husband's face. "What is it?" she asked, in an urgent whisper.

"That little Jackal! That wicked little Jackal!" roared Njobvu. "Look at my bag of honey!"

The Elephant's Wife looked. She pounced on the bag of plaited reeds and picked it up. "Empty!" she screamed, "It's empty! What has happened to the honey?"

"That clever little Jackal has eaten it. That's what has happened to the honey. I see it all now!" Njobvu snorted with anger. "Oh, the cunning of the little creature with his sobs and tears and lying stories of his dear, dead father's kindness! The wickedness of it! Njobvu told his wife exactly what had happened. "What are we to do?" he asked, as his tale came to an end.

The Elephant's Wife considered for a moment, then: "I'll tell you what we will do," she said slowly. "To-morrow morning you will go and search for more honey and I will call on that clever little Jackal. Perhaps he will wish he hadn't been quite so clever!" The voice of the Elephant's Wife had never sounded quite so steely and full of menace before and, angry as he was, Njobvu could not help feeling a tiny spark of sympathy for the clever little Jackal. After all, honey was *so* good, *so* golden, *so* sweet. It was worth almost anything . . . almost. . . . Njobvu looked at his wife again and shook his head. Poor little Jackal!

4

THE CERVAL'S SECRET NAME

"WITHOUT an axe, we cannot clear the land," said Kalulu, the Rabbit.

"And if we cannot clear the land, we cannot have a garden," Njiri, the Warthog, pointed out.

"And if we have no garden, we cannot grow beans," sighed the Antelope.

"Or pumpkins," said the Rabbit.

"Or sweet potatoes," added the Bushpig.

"And if we cannot grow beans . . ."

"Or pumpkins . . ."

"Or sweet potatoes . . ."

"We shall starve!" They finished in chorus and gazed first at each other and then at the site they had chosen for a garden.

It was a fine site with good, rich soil and near enough to the river to survive a drought, but it was covered with trees and shrubs and long grass and before it could be hoed it must be cleared. And without an axe, how could they cut down the shrubs and trees?

"Where can we get an axe?" Kalulu asked.

"Cerval has an axe," said Warthog, "but I don't think he would lend it."

"Not he!" Kalulu snorted with scorn. "He's the meanest creature alive!"

"Perhaps if he knew how badly we needed it . . . " began Antelope.

"And if we were to offer him some of the beans we would grow."

"Or pumpkins."

25

"He doesn't eat beans or pumpkins," Kalulu was quite clear on that point.

"Or sweet potatoes?" asked Bushpig hopefully. He was fond of sweet potatoes and always liked to hear of animals who were not.

"Or sweet potatoes."

"Oh, dear, that does make it difficult!" They all looked very glum.

"I suppose we could ask if he would lend us his axe," Kamba the Tortoise, suggested after a while. "It couldn't do any harm."

"If he has just had a good dinner, he *might* agree." Njiri did not sound very optimistic.

"It really is the only thing we can do," they all said together.

"Very well, then. Antelope shall take the message because he runs more swiftly than we do."

"You'd be much more persuasive, Kalulu!" Antelope was not at all anxious to be the messenger.

"No, Antelope. You are an excellent messenger. You must be the one to go."

And so the Antelope went.

While he was gone, the other animals sat down and discussed their plans for the garden. In this way the time passed quite quickly and they had just decided how many rows of beans there were to be and how many of pumpkins and of sweet potatoes, when Antelope came racing back.

"He's agreed!" he panted excitedly. "Cerval has agreed!"

"He has?" The animals leapt to their feet, scarcely daring to believe their ears. "He is going to lend us his axe?"

"Yes. All we've got to do is to guess his secret name."

"O-o-oh!" A long, drawn-out groan greeted this announcement and they all sat down. "That's a lot of good. We might have known he'd think of something impossible like that. He *is* mean!"

For a long time they sat in gloomy silence.

At length! "There's nothing for it! We've got to guess his secret name," said Kalulu, the Rabbit.

"Yes, but how?"

"Let me think." Kalulu put a paw to his head and closed his eyes. "There must be some way of finding out," he muttered. "There's got to be a way. Supposing we were to . . . no, that's no good. . . . Perhaps if we could surprise him somehow . . . but how? How? . . . Ah! That's an idea! It might work. I do believe it is worth trying!"

"You've got a plan, Kalulu?" Tortoise, Antelope, Warthog and Bushpig all spoke together. They could tell from the look on his face that he was working out some scheme.

"I don't know. It may not work, but I think it is worth trying." Kalulu spoke slowly. "What we must do is to go into the jungle and when we find one of Cerval's traps with a bird in it, we must take out the bird. Then we must go to the river and, when we find a trap with a fish in it, we must take out the fish and put the bird in its place. Then we go back to the snare in the jungle and put the fish in it and hide ourselves and wait and watch what happens when Cerval comes to look at his traps this evening.

"I don't see what good that can do," said Bushpig, voicing the thoughts of all the other animals.

Kalulu grinned at them.

"Wait and see," he said.

*   *   *   *   *

A little track wound through the jungle to the river and in a tangled patch of scrub beneath a Muula tree, the Cerval had set his snare. It was cunningly made of twigs and twine and had achieved its purpose for, when

27

Kalulu and his friends passed by, in it they found a foolish young partridge who had been caught by one of his red legs.

The Partridge fluttered his wings in agitation. "Set me free," he cried as soon as he saw the Rabbit. "Please set me free and I will do anything you ask."

"You could be a great help to us," said Kalulu, and he told him of the garden they longed to make and the condition upon which Cerval had agreed to lend his axe.

"I want you to come with us and let us put you in a fish trap."

"Oh," cried the Partridge in great alarm. "If I do that I shall be killed!"

"No. I and my friends will see that you come to no harm."

"Well, if you are quite sure" . . . the Partridge sounded far from happy.

Kalulu nodded and set the Partridge free and, together, they all walked on until they came to the river. It did not take them long to find a fish trap and in it, happily, there lay a shining silver fish. Carefully Kalulu took it out and, in its place, he put the Partridge and he fixed the trap so that only the Partridge's red legs were in the water. Then he told Tortoise and Warthog and Bushpig to hide in the reeds and to wait and watch what happened.

"And see that no harm comes to Partridge," he added as he wrapped the fish in some damp grass and hurried off with Antelope to the snare in the jungle. When he reached it, he placed the shining silver fish inside it and then he and Antelope hid themselves in the long grass and crouched down to wait.

Bye and bye they heard voices. Excitedly they nudged each other and froze into immediate stillness as the Cerval's two sons came into view, their sinuous long bodies gleaming in the shafts of sunlight that filtered through the trees.

"Beneath the Muula tree," the one was saying. "That's where Father said the snare would be . . . yes, there it *is* and there is something in it."

"Look! Look! A fish!" The young Cerval's voice was shrill with amazement. "By the secret name of our father, Njusi, how can such a thing be?"

Kalulu and Antelope scarcely dared to breathe.

"A fish in a bird-trap! It is not possible. The thing must be bewitched!"

"Don't touch it!" The Cerval's sons were greatly afraid. Fear showed in their wicked little eyes and every whisker twitched with apprehension.

"Don't touch it! Let us go quickly to the river and make sure that all is well with the fish-trap. Let us get away from here!"

With a final frightened glance at the innocent silver fish, the two young Cervals raced off to the river.

Kalulu and the Antelope turned to each other as soon as they had gone. "Did you hear?" They whispered. " 'Njusi'. That must be Cerval's secret name. Now he will have to lend us his axe!" They jumped up and began to dance with glee. "Now we can have our garden, they chanted, "our beans, our pumpkins and our sweet potatoes. Njusi! Njusi! Cerval's secret name!"

Meanwhile, sitting uncomfortably in the reeds, Tortoise, Warthog and Bushpig were feeling bored and

wishing that something would happen when suddenly they heard a commotion and saw the Cervals come racing down the river bank. Excitedly they nudged each other and held their breath.

"Look!" screeched one of the Cervals, as they reached the water's edge. "Look! A Partridge in the fish-trap!"

"By the secret name of our father, Njusi, how can such a thing be?" The second Cerval spoke in a terrified whisper. "Our traps are bewitched! Ai! Ai! What shall we do?"

"Let us get away from here, before a worse thing happens. Let us go home and tell our father of this terrible affair."

Away went the frightened Cervals, while Tortoise, Warthog and Bushpig held their sides for fear of laughing aloud. Then up they jumped, danced up and down with delight and ran to the fish-trap.

"Did you hear?" they asked the Partridge as they set him free. Cerval's name must be Njusi. Now we can have his axe to clear our garden. Now we can have our beans, our pumpkins and our sweet potatoes! Clever Kalulu! Let us hurry and tell him how well his plan has worked!"

* * * * *

At the chosen site for the garden all the animals were assembled and stood chattering in excited little groups. The news had got about that Cerval had agreed to lend his axe to clear the land, provided Kalulu and his friends could guess his secret name. Cerval was to come at midday and, in the presence of them all, Kalulu, the Rabbit, would make his all-important guess.

Not for one moment did Cerval dream the guess would be correct, but the strange happenings at the traps had made him nervous and, when midday came and he approached the circle where Kalulu stood, his walk seemed less confident than usual and he wore an anxious look. Behind him walked his two sons, carrying the axe. This they laid on the ground. The little groups of animals split up and they all crowded round, silent now and tense with expectation, as Kalulu and the Cerval faced each other.

Kalulu bowed. "O Cerval," he began, in his most ceremonious manner, "you have said that you will lend your axe if we can guess your secret name?"

"Thus have I spoken," replied Cerval, "and I will keep my word."

"Is it perhaps 'Mpaka'?"

"No."

"Is it perhaps 'Nkhwangwa'?"

"No." The Cervals were smiling with confidence.

"Is it perhaps 'Njusi'?"

Speechless, the Cerval stared at the Rabbit and a great cry went up from Cerval's sons. "Ai! Ai!" they moaned. "Kalulu knows our father's secret name! Our traps are bewitched! Our power is gone! What will happen to us next? Ai! Ai!"

"When you give me your axe, the spell will be broken. I, Kalulu, who know your secret name, have said so." Never before had the Rabbit sounded so impressive or spoken with such authority. His friends all gazed at him in admiration, while the Cervals stood, bewildered and half-dazed with fear. All that mattered to them now was that the spell should be removed.

At length the Cerval spoke. "The axe is yours," he said. "It shall be as you say." And Cerval made a sign to his sons.

In silence they handed the axe to Kalulu, then turned and walked unsteadily away.

The moment they had gone, all the animals began to cheer and clap and shout.

"Well done, Kalulu! Now we can clear the land. Now we can have our garden, our beans, our pumpkins and our sweet potatoes! Now we shall not starve!"

"What did Cerval's sons mean about the traps being bewitched?" asked one of the animals.

"I can't imagine," replied Kalulu, running his paw along the blade of the axe to test its sharpness.

"They say there was a fish in the bird-trap and a partridge in the fish-trap," explained the Mole.

"Then the traps *must* have been bewitched. How else could such a thing happen?"

"How else indeed?" Kalulu grinned and swung the axe. A little later the first tree came crashing to the ground. The garden was being cleared.

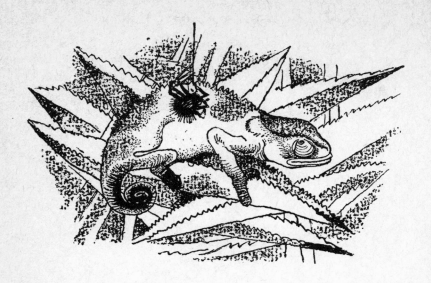

5

THE GREEDY SPIDER

WHAT'LL I do? What'll I do?" cooed the Wood
Pigeon in the top branches of a tall Mlombwa
tree, not because she was in trouble of any kind,
but because she was a foolish bird and never knew what
she wanted to do next.

"As if anyone cares what she does, so long as she stops
making that silly noise," muttered the Spider, who was
hidden away in a crack of the tree trunk. "Now I shall
miss hearing what the Ants have to say . . . miss hearing
any important piece of news for certain!"

It was a boast of the Spider's that he knew everything
that was going on and he made it his business to hide in
unexpected places and listen to what everyone had to
say. Most particularly did he listen to the Bees, who
travelled far and wide and brought news from the
furthest places, and to the Ants, who were very, very
wise and knew all sorts of secrets.

"They say there is to be a feast at . . ." The Ants began to whisper.

"What'll I do?" cooed the Wood Pigeon. "Coo, coo! What'll I do?"

"Oh, bother that bird!" spluttered the Spider. "I didn't hear where the feast is to be. How exasperating! Now, how can I find out?"

Spider was infuriated. If there was one thing he liked to know more than another, it was every single detail concerning a feast, for he was a greedy Spider, a fat, round, greedy Spider, the Great-Great-Grandfather of all the Spiders that ever were. And he dearly loved a feast.

"I wonder if Chameleon knows where the feast is to be held? He might. I think I'll go and see." With practised art, the Spider spun himself a silvery silken thread, ran down it to the ground and scuttled away as fast as he could to the clump of aloes where he knew Chameleon was most often to be found.

The aloes were in flower.Tall, coral-coloured blooms like branching candles, flaming above their blue-grey sword-like leaves. The leaves were edged with spines, very useful and convenient for Spider as points to which a web could easily be thrown. Useful, too, to the Chameleon, for they discouraged quite a number of creatures whom he disliked from coming to see him. Not that it was easy to see Chameleon, because he was so clever at changing his colour and looking like an aloe leaf, if that happened to be where he was sitting. Spider had to look very carefully before he discovered that it was.

"Good morning, Chameleon," he said. "I hope you are quite well? You have breakfasted well, I trust? You will be going to the feast, I presume?"

Slowly Chameleon swivelled his eyes in Spider's direction. "To which feast are you alluding,?" he drawled. "I understand that there are to be several feasts."

"Are there indeed," thought Spider to himself. "That's news to me, but I am not going to let Chameleon see

35

that I didn't know.". Aloud, he said carelessly: "So I understand. No doubt I shall be seeing you then!" and he hurried away just as quickly as he had come.

Chameleon looked a little surprised at this abrupt departure. "Odd," he thought, "very odd!" and with slow, deliberate movements he climbed up the stem of the aloe until he reached the topmost spike of blossom. Here his coat turned to a reddish shade, to match the trumpet-shaped flowers, and he looked around. There was nothing to be seen save the long grass, the tall red candles of the aloes and, far away, the Mountain looking cool and blue and beautiful through the shimmering haze of heat. Spider was out of sight.

He was making for his home, his quick brain scheming busily. What he must do, he decided, was to send for his children and find out where and when the feasts were to be held. The children—some of them—would be sure to know and all he had to do to call them was to beat his drum in a certain way and, wherever they were, they would hear the summons and come hurrying home.

Spider's drum was hidden in the corner of the cave in which he lived. It did not take him long to get there and soon the sound of the drum could be heard throbbing, faintly in the distant places, loud and clear nearby.

"Rat-a-tat, rat-a-tat, rat-tat, rat-tat,
Rat-a-tat, rat-a-tat, rat-tat-tat."

The Spider's children heard it and, wondering what it could mean, hastened to obey the summons. Eagerly the Spider awaited their arrival and, as soon as the first young Spider reached the cave, he asked if there was to be a feast in the Southern district where he lived.

"Yes, father," replied the young Spider. "Kalulu, the Rabbit, is holding a feast, but I do not know when it is to be. Perhaps when the moon is full, perhaps the previous night. I do not know. But it will be a fine feast."

"M'm," said the Spider, licking his lips in a very

36

greedy way. "No doubt it will be a fine feast and I should like to attend it. It is a pity that you do not know exactly when it is to be. However, that difficulty can be overcome. I have a plan. That is what we will do." As he spoke, the Spider began to spin a long, strong, silken thread. One end he wound tightly round his middle and the other end he gave to his child.

"Take this thread, my child, and wind it round yourself as I have done. Then go back to your home and, as soon as the feast is about to begin, pull on the thread and I will come and together we will attend Kalulu's feast. Is that not a good plan?"

"That is a splendid plan, father!" The young Spider gave a delighted laugh. "I had not thought to attend the feast!"

"Aha!" chuckled the Spider. "You youngsters don't know how to enjoy life. You don't know how to look after yourselves. I *always* attend feasts!"

When the second child arrived, Spider asked the same question as he had before and learnt that the Antelopes, who lived in the wooded country to the East, were planning to hold a feast, but the time of the feast had not been fixed and the second child did not know which night it was to be.

"No matter," said his father, and quickly spun another silken thread and wound one end round himself and gave the other to the second young Spider, saying:

"Take this thread, my child, and wind it round yourself as I have done. Then go back home and, as soon as the Antelopes' feast is about to begin, pull on the thread and I will come and together we will attend the feast."

"Oho!" laughed the second young Spider. "What a splendid plan!" and did his father's bidding.

From his third child, Spider learnt that the Bull-frogs, who lived in the Western marshes, were proposing to hold a feast, perhaps when the moon was full, perhaps the following night. And the fourth child said that there was a rumour in the Northern hills that Nyalugwe, the Leopard, was preparing a magnificent feast, but no one knew precisely when it was to be. So Spider spun two more silken threads and wound them round himself and gave the other ends to the third child and to the fourth child, telling them to wind them round themselves as he had done, and to return to their homes and to pull on the threads as soon as the feasts were about to begin.

The children scuttled away and Spider climbed into his favourite web and settled down to sleep. As he dozed, he smiled, and every now and then he licked his lips and muttered greedily, "Four feasts! Four beautiful feasts! And I shall attend them all because I am so clever!"

Golden-red, the full moon rose; the formless dark took shape. The black still waters of the lake turned slowly to a molten glassy sea; the shadows deepened to a richer violet hue; trees, grasses, flowers and ferns took on a silver sheen and, for a breathless moment, everything seemed hushed and still. Then suddenly a drum began to throb, and another, and another, and another. They were beating in the grassy plains of the South, where Kalulu, the Rabbit, had his home; beating to summon Kalulu's guests to the Feast of the Full Moon. The first young Spider heard them and tugged excitedly at the silken thread wound round his waist. Then he began to scurry towards the place where the feast was to be held.

Away to the East, in the wooded country where the Antelopes lived and roamed, another drum began to beat; and another, and another and another. The Antelopes' feast was beginning and the second young Spider heard the drums and tugged excitedly at *his* silken thread and ran towards the sound.

The beating of the drums in the Western marshes, where the Bull-frogs lived, seemed no more than the echo of the throbbing toms-toms in the South and East, while the drums beating in the distant Mountains of the North for the feasting of the Leopards, seemed no louder than the beating of one's heart. The third young Spider and the fourth young Spider listened for a moment, then they, too, tugged at their threads and hurried to the feasts.

"Aha!" chortled the Spider as he felt the tug of his first child's thread. "Kalulu's feast at last!" and he took a step towards the South.

"Ooh!" cried the Spider, as a tug jerked him sharply to the East. "Not two feasts on the same night? What a mistake! What a shame! How can I possibly go to both?"

"Oh, my!" gasped the Spider, as he felt the strong pull of his third child's thread and lurched towards the West. "Three feasts on one night! Whoever heard of such a thing? Whatever shall I do!"

"Ow!" yelled the Spider, as the fourth child dragged him towards the North. "This is terrible! Help! Help!" he shrieked as all four children tugged and the threads tightened round his waist. What was he to do? Try and break three of the threads and only go to one feast? But then to which feast should he go? Leopards' would be the most sumptuous but Kalulu's was nearer and could be reached more easily.

Tighter and tighter grew the threads. Smaller and smaller grew the Spider's waist. He must make up his mind—the pressure was becoming unendurable. He was beginning to feel queer . . . very queer . . . faint . . . ill . . . dizzy.

At that moment the four threads snapped. Spider rolled over once and lay, unconscious, on his back; unconscious of the drums that throbbed on far into the night; unconscious of his anxious children who were scuttling back to find out what had happened to their father.

It was dawn before they reached him and many days before he felt quite well again. But his waist never recovered and all Spiders ever since have had absurdly small waists. This has not cured their greed, however, and they still come if they can, uninvited, to every feast that is held.

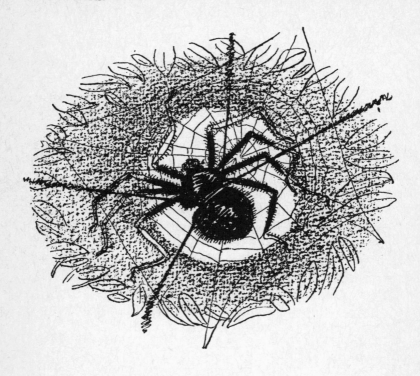

6

THE RAM AND THE LEOPARD

ERFECT! An ideal site! There could not be a better place—quiet, secluded, good shelter from the sun and wind, and water in the stream below. I shall build myself a house here."

Bira, the Ram, was delighted and, indeed, he had reason to be, for he had chosen well. A little knoll rose high above the jungle and, near the top, a level patch of grass offered a perfect site on which to build. Tall trees spread their gracious branches over the place, rocks gave protection from the wind and rain, while a clump of purple vetch proved that the ground was sweet. No wonder the Ram was pleased that his search for a building site in an unknown stretch of country had been so handsomely rewarded.

Determined to lose no time in getting to work, Bira shouldered his axe and hurried back to the forest for he knew that the first thing he must do, if he wished to build a house, was to cut some fine straight poles.

He had not been gone long when Nyalugwe, the Leopard, approaching from the eastern side, climbed up the knoll on to a rock and found himself gazing down on the little grassy patch that lay, snug and invitingly, below.

"What a charming spot," said he, whiskers twitching with appreciation. "An ideal site for a house. Indeed, I think I'll build a house here. It is a most delightful place!"

Nyalugwe considered for a moment. Building a house meant a lot of hard work and he did not like hard work. But he wanted a house and he had never seen a better site, so, having made up his mind, he went back to find an axe with which to cut some poles.

Blip . . . blip . . . ber-lip! Down came a sapling, felled by Bira, the Ram. Carefully he trimmed it, lopping off the branches, lifted it and carried it up to the grassy patch and laid it down beneath a rock. Then he returned to cut another pole.

In another part of the forest, Nyalugwe, the Leopard, swung his axe, blop . . . blop . . . ber-lop! and down came a sapling which he trimmed and carried to the knoll. And he was about to lay it down in the shade of a tree when he saw that one pole already lay beneath a rock.

"Well!" he exclaimed. "What a bit of luck to find that here! It will do splendidly for my house." And Nyalugwe laid his pole beside the first one and ambled off to cut a second tree.

Blip . . . blip . . . ber-lip! Another sapling fell and Bira, the Ram, trimmed it and carried it to the site, put it down, looked at the three poles and scratched his head in a bewildered sort of way.

"Surely I've only cut one pole—or have I cut two? I suppose I must have, for there they are!" Bira was extremely puzzled but he wasn't going to waste time just because his memory was unreliable. Off he went to the forest to cut a fourth tree.

Blop . . . blop . . . ber-lop. "Whew!" said Nyalugwe, the Leopard, as he mopped his brow. "Warm work, this!" and he had a short rest before carrying the sapling to the building site. "That's three poles cut," thought Nyalugwe and, sure enough, three poles were

lying on the ground. Yes, but he was still carrying a pole!

"One, two, three, and one I'm holding. But that's *four* poles! How can this be?" He put the fourth pole down and looked at it hard. Then he started counting again. "One, two, three . . . still four. Have I cut four poles? No!" Nyalugwe was quite sure about this, so he tried to think of some explanation of the mystery.

43

The obvious one was that the place was bewitched—
a most alarming thought and quite the last thing he
wanted to believe. There must be some other explanation. Nyalugwe sat down quickly and thought again and
soon an answer presented itself. The Spirits of his
Ancestors had come to help him! Of course that was it.
What could be more likely? Naturally his Ancestors
would wish to help him build his house.

Greatly relieved and comforted, Nyalugwe jumped
up and hastened off to cut more poles. With the Spirits
of his Ancestors to help him he'd have enough to build
a house in no time at all!

"Four poles! Four poles!" sang Bira, the Ram, as he
climbed up the site and laid his latest sapling down.
"One, two, three, four, . . . oh, my! FIVE!"

Bira sat down abruptly and gazed at the five poles.
He didn't like it. The place must be bewitched! But
that was the last thing he wanted to believe and he
hurriedly remembered that bewitchings never did anyone a good turn like helping them to cut poles so, of
course, that could not be the explanation.

"By the Spirits of my Ancestors, I wish I knew what
to think!" he exclaimed. And, as if in response to this
request, the Spirits of his Ancestors supplied the
answer.

"Of course! It is they who have come to help me.
What could be more likely?" Bowing his head in reverent
gratitude, and greatly cheered by his Ancestors' concern
for his welfare, Bira, the Ram, jumped up and returned
to his work with renewed vigour.

By the time that night had fallen, there were sufficient
poles stacked on the grassy patch to build a fine big
house, and as Bira, the Ram, lay sleeping after his long
day's work, he dreamed of a hundred snow-white Rams
wielding a hundred shining axes and felling trees that
reached from the forest to the stars. And in his sleep he
smiled happily, for it was wonderful to see his Ancestors

all working so hard and to know that they were helping him.

Nyalugwe, the Leopard, also smiled in his sleep as he dreamed of a hundred Leopards, more spotted and more beautiful than any he had ever seen, and some were felling trees and some were cutting grass and some were actually building a house, and in the middle of the house, one Leopard, the handsomest of all, sprawled in idle grandeur and Nyalugwe knew that this Leopard was himself.

Next day, Bira, the Ram, rose early and cut some bundles of tall grass with which to thatch the house and when he reached the building site, he was amazed and delighted to find that the Spirits of his Ancestors had already been at work and that the first poles for the framework of the house were standing in the ground. Inspired by their example, Bira quickly erected the remaining poles, then went away to fetch more grass.

Hardly had he gone when Nyalugwe returned. He, too, had risen early, come straight to the site and, after knocking a few poles into the ground, had gone off to get himself a drink, secretly hoping that while he was away his Ancestors would continue the work and do at least as much as he had done. Nor was he disappointed. His Ancestors had, apparently, completed the framework of the house and had also cut some grass. This Nyalugwe began to weave between the poles to form the walls, but he soon got tired and went away again, hoping that his Ancestors would finish the job.

They did. Before long, Nyalugwe found that if he came early in the morning and did a little work or brought some grass or bamboos for the roof, he could then go away for the rest of the day and his Ancestors would carry on. And each morning, Bira, the Ram, overjoyed to find that his Ancestors had not neglected him but had done a little work or provided something for the house, toiled hard all day so that, by the end of the week, the last bundle of thatch had been laid in place and the house was ready to be slept in.

The Ram looked at it with pride.

"O my great and noble Ancestors," he said. "This is a fine house that we have built and I am very grateful for your help." And he walked three times round the house, then went inside and lay down and soon he was fast asleep.

Bye and Bye, Nyalugwe, the Leopard, came to see if the house was finished. It was almost dark, but even in the half-light he could see what a fine building it was. He walked round it several times, admired it greatly and decided that there was no reason why he should not sleep there.

He went inside. It was quite dark and as Nyalugwe felt weary, he lay down and fell asleep. And as he slept he dreamed. He dreamed again of the hundred Leopards, more spotted and more beautiful than any he had ever seen, and they were dancing round a house. Inside the house there lay a form he could not clearly see. At first he thought it was himself—he was sure it was himself— but no, for as he looked it changed, its spots vanished and he saw that it was a Ram. And suddenly he felt afraid and tried to cry aloud. . . .

Bira, the Ram, was sleeping peacefully and dreaming of his hundred snow-white Ancestors. They were sitting in a circle waiting for someone to come out of a house, and Bira found himself wondering who that someone could be. Was it himself? If not, then who? WHO? The suspense became intolerable, more than he could bear. He *must* know who was inside the house. With a tremendous effort he cried aloud: "Come out, whoever you are!" but all he could manage was an odd, strangled sound and he woke up.

He could still hear that queer cry ringing in his ears. Then, suddenly he became aware that he was not alone in the house. The cry was real. It had been made by something in there with him. He peered into the darkness and felt, rather than saw, the form crouching there. For a moment he thought he must still be dreaming, so he pinched himself to make sure and let out a loud "Ow!" when he found that he was wide awake.

"Oh!" gasped Leopard, also wide awake and now very much alarmed. "Who are you?"

"What are you doing in my house?"

"I am Nyalugwe, the Leopard, and this is *my* house."

"It is not. It is *my* house. I, Bira, the Ram, built it."

"How dare you say so! I cut poles, I cut grass, I . . . ."

"Nonsense!" interrupted the Ram. "I cut poles and grass and I built the house. I and my Ancestors."

"You and your Ancestors, my spots!" exclaimed the Leopard rudely. "Who knocked the first pole into the ground?"

"Well, who did?"

"I did," said Nyalugwe triumphantly. "It is my house."

"*You* knocked the first pole into the ground? You? Not my Ancestors?" Bira, the Ram, was beginning to understand what had happened. "And who put in the other poles? Who put the thatch on the roof?"

"I did, of course," said Nyalugwe.

"You? Are you sure?"

"Well, it wasn't exactly I. My Ancestors did a bit, but that is the same thing."

"Would it interest you to know that it was I who first found the place, I who cut the first pole, I who did almost all the work, I who thatched the roof, I who . . ."

"But it can't have been. You are not my Ancestor!" Leopard felt he had scored a very clever point.

"I should hope not!" snorted the Ram. "But get this into your head. I got here first and I did most of the work, so it is my house."

"Well, I'm going to live in it," said Nyalugwe with a nasty snarl.

"Who's going to live in what?" asked Kalulu, the

47

Rabbit, who had been looking for his friend, Bira, for several days and had at last tracked him down. "My! My!" said he. "This is a very fine house. Is it yours, Bira?"

"Yes," replied the Ram. "I built it. The trouble is that Nyalugwe claims it is his because he cut a few poles and knocked the first one into the ground. But I got here first, I cut the first pole and I did most of the building, so it is mine, isn't it?"

"I think you had better tell me the whole story."

Kalulu listened carefully to everything that Bira and Nyalugwe had to say, then made his pronouncement. "If you have both had a share in the building of the house, you will both have to live in it."

"What? Me live with Leopard?" Bira didn't like the idea at all.

"What? Me live with Ram?" Nyalugwe asked in disgust. He considered himself far too superior to share a house with the Ram.

"Yes. I am sure you will get on very well together," Kalulu said. "And now I must be going. Perhaps, Nyalugwe, you will walk a little of the way back with me? I should like to have a word with you. Goodbye, Bira. I shall come and see you again. I am sure you are going to be very happy in your house."

Bira looked quickly at Kalulu. Had he said "your" new house with just the faintest emphasis, or was that imagination? Suddenly the Ram felt his spirits rise for, as he looked at Kalulu, the Rabbit grinned, closed one eye and gave an unmistakable wink. Then he turned and strolled down the knoll, accompanied by Nyalugwe, the Leopard.

At first they talked of this and that and the weather and they agreed that it looked like rain. Then Kalulu made some complimentary remarks about the new house.

"You will find Bira a very nice fellow to live with," he added. "I am sure you will get on extremely well, but there is one thing you want to watch. He does sometimes fly into terrible rages—very seldom, of course. It is hard to understand the reason for it—some little thing upsets him, I suppose. Well, he flies into a rage, lowers his head and charges straight at the nearest person. He is really dangerous then and could easily kill you."

"Oh, how dreadful! I'd no idea!"

"I thought that you hadn't. But don't let it worry you. Just take care not to upset him in any way and everything will be all right. He is a most delightful fellow, really. Anyway," the Rabbit added reassuringly, "you can always tell when he is going to charge, because he starts going backwards first. Then he kind of pulls himself together before he comes at you. So my advice to you is, if ever you see him going backwards, get out of his way as quickly as you can."

"I will! Indeed I will!"

There was no doubt that Nyalugwe was greatly dismayed to learn of this dangerous trait in the Ram's character and the more he thought about it, the more worried he became. He scarcely dared to take his eye off Bira for a moment and once, when the Ram took a step backwards to avoid treading on a thorn, Nyalugwe's heart missed three beats and he leapt on to a rock above the house.

"Whatever is the matter?" enquired Bira, very much surprised. "Something alarmed you?"

"N-n-no! No. I just felt like jumping," said Nyalugwe, and quickly leapt up and down again to show how true this was.

Twice more that day, when Bira took a backward step, the Leopard jumped on to a rock.

"I wish you wouldn't do that," said the Ram. "It fidgets me!"

"Oh, dear," thought Nyalugwe immediately, "now I have upset him," and he went and sat outside the house and moodily gnawed his claws.

A sudden clap of thunder, followed by torrential rains sent Leopard racing into the house again and, while Bira anxiously watched the storm, wondering if his precious house would be damaged or washed away, Nyalugwe crouched nervously in a corner and watched the Ram.

The storm passed. The sun came out and turned the rain drops on the leaves to glittering jewels and Bira, the Ram, emerged from the shelter of his house to see what damage had been done. There was nothing serious —the rain had only served to settle the thatch—but the pathway to the house had become a muddy stream, strewn with loose stones and pebbles. Bira slipped and slithered as he trotted down the slope.

"Hi!" he called out, as Leopard put his head out to see what the Ram was doing. "Be careful how you walk —a lot of loose stones have been washed on to the path."

The warning came too late. With his first step the Leopard dislodged a large stone that went hurtling down the path and bowled the Ram clean over.

"Help!" yelled Bira, as he fell, and "Ow!" groaned Bira as he picked himself out of the mud and tried to stand up. "I told you to be careful, you clumsy great cat. Now look at the mess I am in! I shouldn't wonder if my leg has not been broken!" Gingerly he tested each leg in turn but, happily, found them whole, while Nyalugwe thought to himself, "Oh my, now he *is* angry, now I have upset him indeed," and with anxious eyes he watched the Ram start up the slope. But the path was so slippery that Bira only slid backwards.

"Bother!" he muttered. "I'll never get up here unless I rush it." He slithered down until he came to level ground, then pulled himself together, lowered his head and charged up the slope.

Transfixed with fear, the Leopard watched him come. "He means to kill me," thought Nyalugwe. "This is what Rabbit meant. What did Rabbit say? 'Get out of his way as quickly as you can.' "

One bound on to the rock above the house, one bound down the other side and away raced Nyalugwe. He ran and he ran and he ran until he could run no more and sank exhausted to the ground. There was only one thought in his head—he was not going back. He'd live

in a cave—anywhere—so long as it was nowhere near Bira, the Ram, who might turn nasty at any moment and charge like that. It simply wasn't good enough. No house was worth it. Oh, no, Nyalugwe was never going back.

* * * * *

When Kalulu, the Rabbit, called on the Ram to enquire how his new house had fared in the storm, he listened with great interest to Bira's story of Leopard's extraordinary behaviour.

51

"What do you think can have happened to Nyalugwe?" the Ram asked anxiously.

"I hear he is living in a cave," said Kalulu. "I expect he was frightened by the thunderstorm."

"Oh? Then is the house all mine now?"

"Yes. Nyalugwe is never coming back."

"Not ever? Really never?" Bira gave a happy sigh. "I can't help being glad," he confided. "I didn't like having to share a house with him. Fancy Leopard being frightened by a thunderstorm! Isn't that odd!" Bira shook his head in a puzzled sort of way.

"Maybe it was you he was frightened of!" Kalulu suggested with a grin.

"Don't be so silly!" said Bira. "As if Nyalugwe could be frightened of me!"

7

THE FIRST ZEBRA

SLOWLY the great red African sun rose from behind the distant mountains, dispelling the soft blue mists of dawn that hung about the Lake and bringing warmth and light to the plain where all the animals were feeding.

Elephant was there, busily knocking down a tree, so that he might breakfast off its tender roots. Close by, the Rhinoceros lay, thinking of nothing at all as he chewed and chewed a mouthful of grass that had occupied him for the past ten minutes. Warthog nosed around, while all the other animals—Eland, Gnu, Hartebeest, Bushbuck, Duiker, and countless others—gently cropped the short young grass, pausing from time to time to question their friends or see how high the sun had climbed. It was as though they were waiting for some signal.

In those days the world was very new indeed and none of the animals had horns or fancy coats, but the time had come when these things were to be given to them and they had been told to go, this very day, to the shores of the Lake where, in a great cave, they would find all kinds of coats and horns from which to choose. So it was with eager eyes they watched the sun for, when it had travelled one quarter of the way towards its zenith, it would be time for them to start.

At length the moment arrived and, with one consent, the animals began to move towards the Lake. Only the Zebra took no notice and went on eating as fast as he could.

"It's a great pity Zebra is so greedy!" Kudu remarked to his friend, the Sable Antelope. "He never seems to think of anything but food and he'll scarcely stop grazing to speak to a fellow. Look at him now!"

Sable chuckled.

"Vulgar creature!" was his comment. "It will serve him right if he is late to-day and gets no coat or horns!"

"Perhaps he hasn't noticed the time," suggested Kudu, who had a kind heart. "I'll give him a shout. Hi! You there! Zebra! It is time to go for your horns. Hurry up, or you will be late!"

"Plen'yo'time," mumbled Zebra with his mouth full, and went on eating.

"You see?" said Sable. "No self-respect. No interest beyond food. Why should we bother about him?"

"You are quite right," agreed Kudu, and together they trotted off in the direction of the Lake.

Elephant was one of the first to reach the cave, where he spent a happy hour turning over the different kinds of coats and horns. When he had chosen a pair of Ivory tusks and a dark grey coat with a short tail behind and what looked like a long tail in front, he quickly put them on and hurried away to the nearest tree. He wanted to see if the trunk was really as useful as he thought it was going to be. To his joy, he found that, with it he could reach even the highest branches where the tenderest leaves grew. He found, too, that he could pick up things from the ground without the slightest effort, and he spent several minutes in tossing a fallen branch about and rooted up no less than three young trees for the sheer pleasure of doing so. Then feeling rather hot, he went down to the Lake to bathe and immediately discovered another use for his new trunk. He could squirt water out of it! Delightedly the happy Elephant passed another hour, splashing about, squirting his own back, and inviting his friends, as they left the cave, to come and watch him.

Meanwhile Kudu and Sable were busy making their choice.

"Personally, I want horns to fight with," Sable said, having selected a wonderful silky coat of the richest chocolate shade. "Now these," he continued, taking up a pair of horns which had a fine, sweeping, backward

55

curve, "these are admirable for the purpose, and handsome, too! See how they suit me!" He put them on and strutted to and fro, while all the animals gazed at him in admiration. Then, remembering that his friend Kudu had not yet found the horns he wanted, he returned to help him make his choice.

Kudu had selected an attractive mole-grey coat with white stripes across the back, but he found it difficult to choose his horns.

"You see," he explained, "I seldom want to fight, but I do want something to protect me from things that fall from trees. As you know, Sable, I spend most of my time in the wooded hillocks, and falling branches, not to mention Leopards and things of that sort, that drop on to my neck, are amongst my greatest troubles."

"What about these, then?" enquired Sable, pointing to a magnificent pair of horns like giant corkscrews. Wouldn't these do if you were careful how you put them on?"

"I do believe they would," agreed Kudu excitedly. For a moment he studied them, then placed them so that they would lie along his back when he was running. Eager to test them immediately, he galloped off, with Sable following, to a thickly wooded rise. As he crashed through the underbush, a dead branch came tumbling down, right on to his neck, Instantly the horns caught it and, with a shake of his head, Kudu was able to throw it off.

"Wonderful! You've no idea what a difference these horns make!" Kudu was delighted and as he and Sable trotted back to the feeding ground, it was easy to see how proud they were and pleased with their new possessions.

On their way they overtook the Bushbuck and several of his companions.

"Charming, Bushbuck, charming!" called Sable as they passed. "I wondered who would choose that delight-

ful reddish coat with the white spots. It suits you beauti-
fully!"

When they reached the plain the first animal they saw
was Zebra, and he was *still* eating as greedily as if he
had not had a good meal for a week at least.

"Goodness, Zebra!" exclaimed Kudu. "Are you never
going to stop? Don't you want a coat or horns?"

"Oh, hullo!" said Zebra, looking up for a moment.
"You back again?" Suddenly he noticed their magnificent
appearances. "I say," he continued, staring with amazement, "you do look fine! My, my! I don't know which
I like best. I think I'll get a coat like yours, Sable, and
curly horns like Kudu." And, hurriedly snatching a last
mouthful of grass, Zebra trotted briskly off towards the
Lake.

All the way to the cave he kept on meeting happy
animals returning to the plain, proudly displaying their
lovely coats and horns, and as he passed them they all
called out:

"Hurry up, Greedy, or there'll be nothing left for
you!"

Last of all he met the Rhinoceros, who looked more
peculiar than ever in his ill-fitting coat and odd horns.
Being short-sighted, he had chosen two horns of different
sizes and these he had placed end-wise on his forehead
instead of across. Zebra rudely burst out laughing when
he saw him, but Rhinoceros only blinked his little eyes
and looked the other way.

Still laughing, Zebra entered the cave and looked
about him. It was quite empty except for a vulgar black
and white striped coat with a large mouth and an ugly
drooping lip. Not a single horn was left. For a little
while Zebra stood looking sadly at the coat. Then, half-
heartedly, he tried it on. It fitted perfectly, and the loud
pattern rather appealed to Zebra's common taste. No, it
wasn't bad, and none of the others had anything like it.
And what did horns matter, anyway? Better far to have

a large mouth, even if it had an ugly lip, thought Zebra,
and, feeling quite happy again, he hurried back to the
feeding ground.

But oh, the jeers and laughter that greeted him from
the plain. Even the little Duiker pointed scornfully at
him and cried:

"Look at the greedy Zebra who hasn't any horns!"
And all the animals took up the chorus:

"Look at the greedy Zebra who hasn't any horns!"

But Zebra didn't really care. What did it matter if
everyone jeered at him? What did anything matter so
long as the grass was green and tender and there was
plenty of it for him to eat?

To this day the Zebra is the greediest animal in all
Africa. He doesn't mind a bit about having no horns or
such a strange appearance. All he cares about is

食

food,
Food,

FOOD.

8

THE SPIDER AND THE LIZARD

HUNDREDS and hundreds of years ago, in the middle of Africa, there lived a Spider who thought himself extremely clever. In fact, he thought himself cleverer than anyone else in the world and he gave himself tremendous airs which, of course, made him very unpopular with other animals. The only one who might be considered a friend of Spider's was the Lizard, and this was because they lived near each other and because Lizard was unpopular too. Everyone knew he was a good-for-nothing creature who never did a stroke of work. He just spent his days lying idly in the sunshine, laughing at the Bees, laughing at the hard-working Ants, laughing even at Spider as he spun his web.

"Don't know what you've got to laugh about!" grumbled Spider. "Only a brainless reptile like you would sit about doing nothing but gibe at clever fellows like me who do all the work!"

"Ah! But *I* don't think you are clever," said Lizard.

"I'm the one with brains because I manage to get along very well without doing any work at all!"

"You don't think I'm clever?" Spider spluttered indignantly. "You dare to compare your paltry little brain with mine? You conceited wastrel! You miserable . . ."

"Newz! Newz!" shouted a Bee who flew past at that moment. "Have you heard the newz?"

"What news?" asked Lizard, while Spider was still choking down his fury.

"About the Princess," replied the Bee. "It has just been proclaimed in the Market Place."

"Tell us," said Lizard eagerly, as Bee settled on a blade of grass and Spider crawled near to listen.

"The Proclamation says that whoever guesses the Princess's secret name shall receive her hand in marriage. No one is allowed more than one guess. You never know, you might be lucky! There's a chance for every one of

us. Well, good-bye, I can't stop chatting here all day—
must be getting along and spreading the glad tidings!"
And away flew the Bee, buzzing as he went, "newz!
newz!"

"H'm!" said Lizard thoughtfully. "Only one guess.
You probably wouldn't guess it if you had a thousand."

"*You* certainly wouldn't," snapped the Spider. "But
then you've no brain. Now, a clever chap like me *has* got
a chance. I must go away and think this over." He
crawled away to his favourite thorn tree, while Lizard,
laughing derisively, settled down to sleep in the warm
sunshine.

*   *   *   *   *

The Princess had just finished her evening meal and
lay on a couch, singing softly as her fingers plucked the
strings of a quaint old lyre. The song came to an end and
she sighed, thoughtfully, and murmured to herself, "I
wonder if Kembi will come to-morrow?"

Kembi was a great hunter who had loved the Princess
ever since he first set eyes on her, and when the Princess
saw him at one of the Palace feasts—saw how brave and
handsome he was—she knew she loved him too. Sometimes they were able to meet secretly in the Princess's
garden, but often they did not see each other for long
periods, as Kembi's home lay far distant from the Palace.

In those days it was the custom in all countries to
arrange competitions or contests in which the hand of
the King's daughter was generally the prize. Sometimes
it was a question of killing a dragon, or riding up a glass
mountain, and sometimes it was something not so
dangerous but very nearly as difficult. In the present
case it was the Princess herself who had suggested to her
father that she should be allowed to marry the person
who guessed her secret name, for she knew that the only
one who held the answer was Kembi. She had even sent
a message to him telling him of the Proclamation and

now she was wondering how soon he could reach the Palace and claim her as his bride.

So busy was she with her thoughts that she never noticed that a large Spider had crept into her room and was climbing up into the rafters where he could not be seen.

Presently the curtain of the doorway was thrust aside and the King strode into the room to bid his daughter good-night.

"Well, well," he said jovially, "to-morrow, I suppose, we shall have all sorts of people and creatures coming here to guess your name. But I don't suppose anyone will succeed, for no one here has ever heard the name 'Nyala' before!"

"I wonder!" murmured the Princess.

"Anyway, we'll soon know! Mind you look your best to-morrow, and you had better be ready in the Great Hall an hour after sunrise," said the King. "Good-night, my dear!"

"Good-night, Father," replied the Princess, with a happy smile.

Some minutes later, when the lights had been extinguished and all was quiet in the Palace, Spider crept down from his hiding-place in the rafters and hurried back to his home. He was bursting with excitement and pride at his own cleverness and, as he scuttled over the ground, he thought to himself: "Now I'll be able to show that Lizard what brains can do! . . . I'll go to the Palace first thing in the morning and claim the Princess. . . . 'Nyala' . . . Hm, pretty name! . . . My, how grand I'll be . . . why, I shall be a Prince! . . . A Prince would have Heralds, Ambassadors, at least a Messenger—a Prince would never go to the Palace himself . . . I must have a Messenger . . . I know, Lizard shall be my Messenger! Lizard shall carry my message to the King!" And, instead of going to his own house, Spider went to Lizard's and entered without even bothering to knock.

"Hullo, what's up?" asked Lizard, sleepily opening one eye.

"Get up and bow—and kindly call me 'Sir' in future," was the Spider's reply.

"What?" said Lizard, now wide awake. "*Me* bow? *Me* call *you* 'Sir'? You know, you can't be well!"

"I know the Princess's name," announced the Spider pompously, "and I wish you to take a message to that effect to the Palace."

"Oho!" said Lizard, looking very cunning. "Well, I don't mind doing that to oblige an old friend. But you will have to tell me what the name is or they won't believe you really know."

"Hm," mused Spider, "m'yes, I suppose there is something in that! The name is 'Nyala'. You will deliver the message to the King himself, in the Great Hall, one hour after sunrise. Then come straight back to me. Now, I must be off," added Spider, and turned to go.

"Good-night, *Sir!*" said Lizard, bowing low. Then, as he shut the door behind the Spider he began to laugh, and he laughed and he laughed until the tears rolled down his cheeks and all his scales ached.

Next morning Lizard presented himself at the Palace and was ushered into the Great Hall. Placing his hand on his heart and bowing almost to the ground, he said that he had come to guess the Princess's name. Was it, perhaps, "Nyala"? He waited expectantly.

The Princess could scarcely believe her ears and even the King seemed taken aback. But he admitted that the guess was correct and told Lizard to come again in seven days' time to claim his bride.

The Court was then cleared and Lizard left the Palace, but he did not go back to the Spider or to his old home. He went to a hiding place he knew of in quite a different direction. The news of Lizard's triumph, however, travelled like lightning and soon reached

Spider, who was waiting impatiently for his Messenger's return. When he realised how he had been tricked, Spider's rage knew no bounds, and he decided to go straight to the Palace and tell the King all that had happened.

The King was very angry—angry with Spider for eavesdropping and furious with Lizard for his deceit. Both creatures were disqualified and banished from the Court, the competition was cancelled and the Princess was permitted to be betrothed to Kembi, the hunter, when he reached the Palace later in the day.

Spider returned home feeling very subdued, and very much afraid that, somehow, he had not been quite as clever as he had thought. But he was determined to be revenged on the Lizard, and Lizard knows it. And that is why the Lizard is so nervous and why he turns his head sharply from side to side, as if he is watching for something. He is. He is watching to see if there is a Spider anywhere about!

9

THE TORTOISE AND THE OSPREY

"WHY can't I fly?" grumbled Kamba, the Tortoise. "Or climb trees? Or . . . "

"For the very good reason that you weren't meant to!" snapped the Tortoise's wife, who had heard all this before and strongly disapproved of her husband's adventurous ambitions.

"But, my dear," he explained, "think what Prestige it would give us!" Tortoise had no idea what "Prestige" meant but he thought it sounded grand and he knew he was safe in trying it on his wife. It ought to impress her.

It did not impress her.

"What's 'Prestige' and why do you want it?" she demanded suspiciously.

"Oh, er . . . er . . . I thought you'd like it, my dear," he stammered lamely.

"Then you thought wrong. I'M quite content with

things as they are, and I haven't time to waste talking
about prestiges and things of that sort. Prestige indeed!"
Tortoise's wife snorted with contempt and bustled off
to her cooking-pots.

Kamba, the Tortoise, looked a little crushed, but only
for a moment. The first few puffs of tobacco from his
ancient pipe restored his confidence and before long he
fell asleep in the hot sunshine, murmuring sadly to
himself, "if only I could fly!"

The reason why Kamba yearned for this accomplish-
ment was that he wished to visit his rich and noble
friend, the Osprey. How the friendship came about it is
hard to say, but no doubt the funny little Tortoise
amused the Osprey who was a happy-go-lucky, kind-
hearted bird, and he often used to drop in at the Tortoises' for a smoke and a chat before returning to his
own home in the tree-tops. And as he was leaving he
would always ask, "When are you going to pay us a
visit, Kamba?" And Kamba would hurriedly say,
"Well, not *this* week, Osprey, old friend, I'm afraid I
am much too busy. But I'll come as soon as I can."

Now if only Tortoise had been honest enough to explain that he had no means of getting to Osprey's home,
all would have been well. But Kamba thought that
Osprey would despise him if he were to say he could
not fly, or climb trees or, in fact, do anything but crawl
along the ground and that very slowly. So Tortoise went
on hoping that he would find a way. The trouble was
that he must find it soon. He could not put off the visit
indefinitely, or Osprey would begin to wonder why.
Then, too, there was the Chameleon who lived nearby
who had guessed what was up and who now never missed
an opportunity of jeering at Tortoise.

"Have you learnt to fly yet, Kamba?" he would call
out. "Have you paid your call on Osprey?" And Tortoise did not know how to avoid him because he never
saw him until he heard his voice.

It was the voice of the Chameleon that now roused him from his pleasant sleep.

"Pity you can't climb trees like me, isn't it, Kamba?" he was saying. He was disguised as a rock this morning and Tortoise had to look twice before he discovered him.

"It's a pity you've got such a long tongue!" retorted Kamba, and he moved off as fast as he could, found another sunny corner, and gave himself up to thought once more.

Suddenly an idea came to him. A brilliant idea! A splendid idea! Tortoise could hardly contain himself at the thought of it and crawled off at top speed to find his wife.

"What's the hurry?" she enquired as soon as she saw him.

"My dear, I have a wonderful idea! I think even you will be pleased with it," replied Tortoise and, as quickly as he could, he told her of his plan.

"H'm!" said Tortoise's wife. "It is not a bad idea . . . and it certainly would be polite to return the Osprey's many calls. And perhaps if you do, you will be more contented. Yes, I don't mind helping you this time. When do you expect Osprey to come here again?"

"I think he will come to-morrow," answered Tortoise. "So we must be prepared."

Sure enough, next morning the Osprey arrived, looking very fine and handsome. Tortoise's wife met him and said how sorry she was that her husband was out. He had had to go visiting, but he had left a present of tobacco for Osprey.

Osprey was delighted, politely said that it was very kind of Tortoise to have given him a present and added that he was sorry not to see him.

"I expect you will see him soon," said Kamba's wife, giving him a bundle of tobacco leaves. It was a very neat bundle, carefully tied up with twine. Osprey took it in his beak, spread his great wings and flew off.

Inside the bundle, of course, was Tortoise, and he was thinking to himself how well his plan had worked and how surprised and pleased Osprey would be to see him when he undid the tobacco leaves. But after a while Tortoise began to feel very hot and uncomfortable and he hoped that Osprey had not got much further to go. But it seemed that Osprey had. Tortoise became more and more unhappy. He decided he did not like flying, that he never would like flying. . . . At last, he could bear it no longer.

"Hi!" he called. "Put me down. I feel . . . "

He never finished his sentence for, at the sound of a voice coming from the middle of a bundle of tobacco leaves, Osprey opened his beak and let out a squawk of terror and his bundle dropped to the ground.

Luckily for Tortoise, Osprey had not been flying very high and the tobacco leaves helped to break his fall. Moreover, he landed on his back, where he had his hard shell to protect him, but it was a very bruised and shaken Tortoise who crept out of what had been the present-for-Osprey, and when he reached his home, he found that his shell was cracked in several places.

Tortoise's wife was not very sympathetic.

"Be thankful it wasn't worse," she said, when she had heard the sad story. "I never really approved of your foolish plan"—which wasn't quite true—"but now, perhaps, you'll be content to stay on the ground for the rest of your days," she finished up.

"Yes, my dear," said Tortoise humbly and crawled to his favourite place in the sun.

"Hullo!" said a clump of red aloes, in which Kamba eventually discovered the Chameleon. "I like your new shell. It *is* handsome with that criss-cross pattern on it."

Tortoise looked at Chameleon and saw that he was quite serious. He tried not to show his surprise as he answered in an off-hand manner, "It is smart, isn't it? I am so glad you like it. Good-bye" and he crept hurriedly back to his wife and told her what Chameleon had said.

"So you see," he chortled happily, "I think I've got Prestige after all!"

"Pouf!"' said his wife. "I don't believe you know what it is!"

All this happened a very long time ago, and as Kamba was the father of all Tortoises, every one of them has criss-cross pattern cracks in his shell.

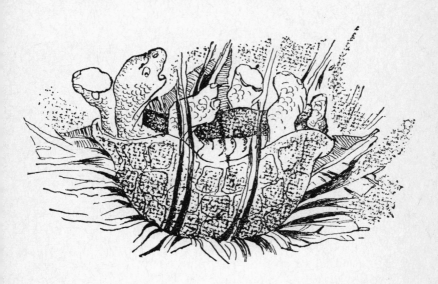

10

KALULU AND THE ELEPHANT

"BEANS?" said the Elephant wistfully, "Who said 'beans'?"

"I did," replied Kalulu, the Rabbit. "I was wishing we had got some. I'm so hungry!"

"Me, too," said the Elephant. "I greatly fear that the time has come when we shall have to work for our food. Are you any good at hoeing?"

"I can manage all right," answered the Rabbit. "And if we have got to work, the sooner we start, the better. Let us go to the Chief of Namadzi. I know he has a great store of beans."

"By all means," agreed Njobvu, the Elephant, "if you are sure about the store of beans?"

So Kalulu and the Elephant set off for the village of Namadzi, which means "by the water", and they asked the Chief to give them work in his fields. This the Chief was glad to do, for he possessed much land, and he also gave them some beans so that they might set them to

cook while they worked and eat them when they had
finished their tasks.

It was very hot in the fields, but Kalulu, the Rabbit,
worked harder than he had ever worked before, because
he was so hungry and wanted his dinner so badly.

Njobvu, the Elephant, did not work quite so hard and kept on stopping and complaining of the heat. Once he left off altogether and went away to pick some banana leaves which he put on his forehead to help to keep him cool; so that by the time Kalulu had finished his task, Njobvu still had quite a lot to do.

"You have been quick!" said the Elephant enviously. "I'm so tired I shall never be able to finish all this!" He waved his trunk dejectedly over the patch of ground that still lay untouched.

Kalulu sighed and looked with longing at the place where the beans were cooking. "I suppose I shall have to help him," he murmured sadly to himself. But aloud he called out, quite cheerfully, "Don't worry! I'll give you a hand." And, wearily. he began to hoe again.

At length the whole task was finished and the friends laid down their hoes and walked over to the beans. How good they looked! How good they smelt!! How good they were going to taste!!! But just as the Rabbit was about to help himself, Elephant said:

"Wait a minute, old fellow. You don't want to start without me and I simply must have a wash first. I feel so hot and dirty. You wait here and keep an eye on the beans, while I go and bathe in the river."

"Very well," sighed Kalulu, with tired resignation. "But don't be long because I'm dreadfully hungry."

The Elephant did not answer for he was already on his way to the river. When he reached the bank, he turned aside into the long grass and hid behind a tall mahogany tree. Then he unbuttoned his coat which, in those days, fastened neatly all down the middle with no less than sixteen buttons, folded it carefully and laid it down on the ground.

Meanwhile Kalulu was sitting by the beans, licking his lips in anticipation, sniffing the delicious smell and hoping that the Elephant would hurry, when, suddenly, he heard a strange roar and, to his horror, he saw a huge and terrifying creature charging down on him. It came from the direction of the river and was like nothing he had ever seen before. It was so big, too. To the frightened little Rabbit it looked almost bigger than an Elephant. Nearer it came and nearer, while poor Kalulu gazed at it in spellbound fascination. Then, when it was all but on top of him, he gave one squeal of terror and fled.

It was some time before he could pluck up enough courage to return and see what was happening and, when he did, he found that the awful creature had disappeared. Cautiously Kalulu crept forward to where the beans had been cooking. There were no beans there! Not a single one had been left!

Miserably Kalulu sat down to await the Elephant's return, and it was not long before he saw him. Evidently the Elephant had had a pleasant time, for he was smiling happily.

"Are the beans ready?" he called out.

"Njobvu!" wailed the Rabbit. "The most awful thing has happened. While you have been away a terrible monster came and ate up all the beans. There are none left for us."

"A terrible monster?" snorted the Elephant, furiously. "I don't believe you! You are cheating me. You've eaten the beans yourself!"

"I haven't. Indeed I haven't," protested Kalulu. "It really was some frightful monster."

"Well," said Njobvu, more calmly, "I suppose I shall have to believe you. We can't get any more beans until to-morrow, so we may as well look for somewhere to sleep. I shall be glad of a good sleep after all that hard work!"

Kalulu said nothing. He was so hungry that he was afraid he would not sleep, even after all the hard work that *he* had done.

Next day the Chief gave Kalulu and the Elephant another task and some more beans. Again the Rabbit worked well and finished before the Elephant and again he had to help Njobvu with his hoeing. Then, when he had completed the tasks, Njobvu went off to bathe, just as he had the previous day and, as Kalulu sat watching the beans, the same fearful monster appeared, scared him away, and ate up all the beans.

When the Elephant returned from the river and Kalulu told him what had happened, he was very angry indeed.

"I don't believe a word of it!" he roared. "You are deceiving me. You've eaten all the beans yourself!"

"I haven't," declared Kalulu, stamping his foot. "And I'll tell you what I am going to do," he continued. "I am going to make a bow and some arrows. Then, if the monster comes to-morrow, I'll kill him!" And Kalulu went off to look for a suitable piece of wood.

That evening Njobvu asked the Rabbit if he had made his bow. Kalulu nodded.

"Let's have a look at it," said the Elephant. "I'm rather an authority on bows and I'll tell you if you have made a good one."

"H'm," he continued, when Kalulu had brought the bow and he had examined it. "Not bad! Not at all bad, but it is too thick here. Still, we can soon put that right." With a sharp flint, Njobvu carefully pared away the wood in one central spot until it was very thin indeed. Then he handed the bow back to the Rabbit. "There you are, Kalulu," he said. "That *is* a good bow now. If the monster comes again to-morrow you should certainly kill it."

Everything happened next day just as it had on the two previous days, and when the monster appeared, Kalulu took his bow and fitted an arrow to it. Immediately the bow broke—just at the place where Elephant had pared the wood away, and so once more the Rabbit ran away and, for the third time, the monster ate up all the beans.

"What luck?" called out Njobvu, as he returned from

his bathe. "Did the creature come and have you killed it?"

"No," answered Kalulu shortly. "The bow broke."

Now if Kalulu had been looking at the Elephant he would have seen a smile spread over his face. But he was not looking. He was thinking very hard and wondering lots of things. Most of all he was wondering what an Elephant looked like without his coat with the sixteen buttons. He wondered so much about this that, on the morning of the fourth day, he got up very early and made himself a new bow. This he hid in the long grass near the place where the beans were to be cooked.

The morning passed off just as usual, but when the Elephant went off to bathe, Kalulu quietly went and fetched his bow and waited. . . .

Soon he heard the monster's roar and, as the creature came in sight, Kalulu took careful aim and loosed an arrow.

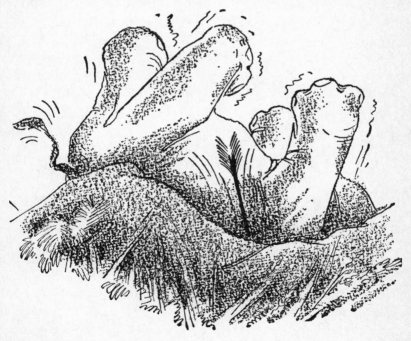

With a scream of pain and rage, the great brute fell.

"Oh, oh, oh!" it moaned. "How could you do such a thing, Kalulu, just for the sake of a few old beans!"

"So it *is* you, Njobvu, who has tricked me each day and made me go hungry!" said Rabbit, in a voice cold with anger and bitter with contempt. "Call yourself a friend, indeed!"

"It was only a joke, Kalulu. I was going to leave some beans for you to-day. But now, see what you have done! You've wounded me and I shall die!" Njobvu burst into loud sobs of self-pity.

"Nonsense," said Kalulu, pulling out the arrow. "Your wound is nothing. Go back to the river, wash it and put on your coat. And never dare to try your tricks on me again!"

Slowly the Elephant struggled to his feet and shuffled away. Kalulu watched him go. Then he turned towards the pot of beans . . . how good they looked! . . . How good they smelt!! . . . How good they tasted!!!

11

THE LEMUR AND THE SHREW

"How lovely! How beautiful! Tell me what it is?" Changa, the Lemur, was addressing his companion, Nsulu, the Shrew, and they were looking at the first bush-fire they had ever seen. It was a long way off and, in the purple stillness of the African night, it seemed as if a whole mountain was ablaze. Other fires on other hillsides danced and flickered, but in the golden glow from the mountain, the stars themselves grew pale and dimmed their gentle light. Spellbound, the Lemur gazed at the sight, while Nsulu scarcely heard his companion's question.

"What is it?" he murmured at last, almost in a trance.

"Why, it is the most wonderful thing I have ever seen! I think it must be Fire."

"What is Fire?" asked Changa, who wasn't very old and who had had no education whatever.

"*That* is Fire," answered the Shrew, pointing to the flaming mountain. "At least, I think so," he finished lamely. He, too, was quite uneducated, but he had heard others talking about fire and he knew vaguely that people made use of fire, and somehow he felt in his bones that what they were looking at *was* Fire. But he didn't know how to explain it to the Lemur.

"I like it. I want some," said Changa after a pause. "Let us go at once and get some for ourselves and then we shall be able to watch it dance every night."

"It is a long way off," began Nsulu doubtfully. "And I'm not sure if we can get any for ourselves."

"Get any what?" asked a voice from behind.

Changa, the Lemur, gave a startled jump. So did the Shrew, and hurriedly turned round to see who it was that had come upon them so silently and suddenly.

"What is it that you want?"asked the voice again, and they saw that the speaker was Kalulu, the Rabbit.

"Don't do it!" exclaimed Nsulu crossly. "You ought to know better than to come sneaking up behind us like that. You made us jump!"

"So I noticed," said Kalulu with a grin. "But you haven't told me yet what it is that you want? Perhaps I can help you."

"We want some of that beautiful fire," replied Changa, waving a paw in the direction of the blazing mountain.

"Don't be silly!" laughed Kalulu. "You can't possibly have that and, if you take my advice, you won't even go near it. Bush-fires may be lovely to look at but they are very unpleasant things to be in. Anyway, what do you want with fire?"

"Er. . . . Well, *people* have fire, don't they? So why shouldn't we?" demanded the Shrew.

"Yes, that is so," agreed Kalulu, stroking his left ear pensively. "I hadn't thought of it like that. Certainly people have fire, and the best thing you can do is to go to the nearest village and see if you can find the remains of fire. Bring back the embers and be sure to keep them glowing and alive!"

"Oh, let's do that," exclaimed Changa, the Lemur. "Where is the nearest village?"

"It was a two nights' lope in that direction," said Kalulu, pointing towards a distant gleam of moonlit water. "But I did hear that the people were thinking of moving. Anyway, you'll soon find out when you get there. Now, if you'll excuse me, I'll be getting along. I haven't had my supper yet. Good-bye and good luck to you!" Kalulu, the Rabbit, waved a paw and vanished as silently as he had come.

"Did he say a two nights' lope?" Changa, the Lemur, sounded a little plaintive.

"Yes," replied Nsulu, the Shrew. "It is a long way, but if we get tired we can always stop and rest."

The Lemur and the Shrew set off towards the distant lake, chattering gaily of this and that, and most particularly of the party they would give when they had a fire of their own. In this way the time passed quickly and they covered a good distance, but by midnight they were scuttling along in silence and when Changa suggested in a small, tired voice that it would be nice to stop and watch the bush-fire for a bit, Nsulu readily agreed.

The moon was setting by the time they were ready to continue their journey. For a while the two friends travelled on, resting now and then, and speaking very little. Gradually the rests grew more frequent and by the time the first grey streaks of dawn were lighting up the sky, too tired to go a step further, they lay down by the pathway and fell asleep.

They slept all through the day, woke as the sun was setting and eagerly resumed their quest. All through the night they walked and stopped and rested and walked again and, at the break of day, two weary little animals crept into a deserted village and sank exhausted to the ground beside the day-old ashes of the chieftain's fire.

It was not until they woke next afternoon that they realised that the fire was past rekindling and that there was no one to tell them where the villagers had gone. They were almost in despair when they saw a slight movement in the thatch of one of the huts.

"Hi!" called out Nsulu instantly. "Is anyone at home there?"

"It all depends on what you mean by 'at home'," answered a voice. "This is not my home, but it has afforded me a convenient temporary refuge. You haven't seen Mongoose, I suppose?".

"No," said the Shrew. "Why?"

"No sensible Rodent cares to emerge from his refuge, however temporary, if there is a Mongoose about," came the pompous reply, and over the side of the hut appeared the head of an elderly, bewhiskered Rat.

"What are you two doing here?" he asked, after he had introduced himself, and somewhat sadly the Lemur and the Shrew told their story.

"Dear, dear, dear!" said Rat, when they had finished. "To think that the people only left here two days ago! That's what I call bad luck! Still, they can't be much more than a two-days' scamper away, can they? And I do know which direction they took."

Shrew looked at Lemur and Lemur looked at Shrew.

"Another two-days' walk!" they both exclaimed unhappily. Then, as if ashamed of their weakness, they pulled themselves together. "What of it?" they said proudly. "It is worth it!" they said, and asked Nkoswe, the Rat, to direct them on their way.

It was after they had been walking for nearly three hours that Lemur gave a sudden squeal of pain and sat down abruptly in the middle of the track.

"Whatever is the matter?" asked Shrew in great agitation.

"Ow!" wailed Changa, clutching at his off hind paw. "A thorn or something. My, how it hurts!"

"Here, let me see," said Nsulu and made a hurried examination. Sure enough, a horrid big thorn had run into the soft part of Changa's paw and when Nsulu tried to pull it out, the thorn broke, leaving the tip firmly embedded in the most tender spot.

"Oh, dear! We'll never get that out now!" Shrew was very much upset. "Do you think you can walk at all?"

"I'll try." Changa, the Lemur, got up, gingerly put his paw to the ground and limped a little way. Shrew watched him anxiously and shook his head as he saw that the little Lemur could not possibly go far.

"No, Changa," he said. "It's no good. You'll have to lie up and wait until the thorn has worked its way out."

"But our fire?" moaned Changa. "We must get our fire!"

"*I* will get our fire. All by myself!" Shrew's voice rang with pride and determination. "You must lie hidden somewhere," he continued. "Look! That tree is the very place. You can see the track from there and you will be quite safe. You will have to watch the track carefully for my return, for perhaps I might forget which tree you were in and miss you. Will you do that?"

Sadly the Lemur agreed. "I want to go with you, but I suppose you are right," he said, and hobbled to the tree.

So it happened that the Shrew journeyed on alone, while Lemur lay curled up in the highest branches, alternately licking his injured paw and watching the track by which his friend would, in time, return.

It was a weary trek for Shrew. All through that night he walked and all through the next, with never a halt, for he was determined to succeed. At length he reached a place where the people he was seeking must have been

encamped for, in a clearing, he found the ashes of many
fires and from one of them a pale wisp of smoke was
slowly drifting upwards to the sky.

Squeaking with excitement, Shrew ran round and
round it, wondering how he was to carry the last glowing
embers back to his friend. And then he found the very
thing—a broken pot! With one piece he scraped the
embers on to another piece, gently blowing at them to

keep them alight. Tired as he was, he immediately began his journey back, and all the while be blew and blew at the precious bits of wood. Even when he stopped to rest he lay so that his breath should fan the spark and keep his little fire alight.

Meanwhile the Lemur, secure in his hiding-place, had scarcely dared to take his eyes off the track for one second in case he should miss his friend. He dared not even sleep and almost welcomed the pain in his paw which helped

to keep him awake. On the fourth day the pain eased and with a final lick, Changa was able to extract the thorn. Hardly had he done so when he saw something scuttling along the track, a small animal, blowing for all he was worth at the thing he was carrying. It looked like Shrew, and yet there was something different. . . .

"Shrew! Shrew! Is that you?" called Changa excitedly.

"Yes, yes! I've got it! Where are you, Changa?"

"Here. I'll be down in a moment." Hurriedly the Lemur climbed down the tree and ran to meet the Shrew. As they came face to face they both stopped dead and stood staring at each other.

85

"What's happened to your mouth?" whispered Changa after a pause.

"What's happened to your eyes?" gasped Nsulu, simultaneously.

"What's the matter with my mouth?"

"What's the matter with my eyes?"

And then they told each other. With all the blowing he had done, Shrew's mouth had grown into the long, funny shape it is to this day. And with all the watching *he* had done, the Lemur's eyes had grown larger and larger and rounder and rounder, until they had become like large black gooseberries.

Did they care? No. They had got their Fire. They could have their party. They had succeeded!

12

THE MUULA TREE

"BY my whiskers," sighed Nkhandwe, the Jackal, "I just can't remember when I last had a good meal, and there doesn't seem to be a thing to eat in these parts!"

Nkhandwe was sitting underneath a Muula Tree, hugging himself tightly so that he should not feel as empty inside as he really was. He had had scarcely anything to eat for days and was beginning to look almost as hungry as he felt. Suddenly he heard a gentle plop and, on looking round, he saw a squishy-squashy fruit lying on the ground beside him. For a moment he gazed at it with unbelieving eyes. Then, licking his lips, he got up and sniffed it very carefully. It smelt good. And it certainly looked good. But did it taste good?

Five seconds later Nkhandwe, the Jackal decided, that it did, but he still wondered if it would give him a poison-pain inside. So he sat down to wait and see, and while he was waiting he gazed hopefully at the branches of the tree which he now saw were heavily laden with ripe fruit. Surely more would drop off soon? . . . More did . . . and more . . . and more . . . and there was not even the faintest squiggle of a poison-pain!

"I must go and tell Kalulu of my find," thought Nkhandwe, having eaten as much as he could manage, and he trotted off briskly to the place where the Rabbit lived. On his way he met Kudu and, being a generous Jackal, he called out: "If you want a good feed, Kudu, I can tell you where to find it."

"Thank you, little Jackal. That is very kind of you."

"Follow the path by which I have come until you reach a big ant-hill. Then turn towards the sun and soon

you will see a tall tree laden with fruit. The fruit is just ripe and is delicious."

"I'm sure it is!" said Kudu, and galloped away.

A little while later Nkhandwe met Njobvu, the Elephant, and, still feeling generous, he told him about the Muula Tree. And later still, while Nkhandwe was telling Kalulu, Njobvu, the Elephant, was telling the Rhinoceros and Kudu was telling Nchefu, the Eland. Soon afterwards Eland told Hartebeest who immediately went and told the Gnu, and goodness knows how many animals Gnu told for, when Mkhandwe and Kalulu returned to the tree, they found it completely surrounded and could not get near to it themselves.

"This is a bad business!" exclaimed Kalulu. He had been accidentally kicked by Bushbuck while trying to get at the fruit.

"You are right," agreed Jackal, who also had been kicked and was busily licking an injured forepaw. "Why did I ever tell anyone about my tree? If only I had had the sense to keep quiet, we could have had the fruit all to ourselves!"

"Well," said Kalulu, "it doesn't look as if we are going to get any now, so we may as well go away and come again early to-morrow morning." The two friends trotted off, leaving the other animals pushing and jostling each other in their efforts to eat the Muula fruit.

Early next morning, so early that the stars had not faded from the sky, Nkhandwe and Kalulu got up and ran to the tree. But Kudu had risen even earlier, and so had Hartebeest and all his friends, and Gnu and all his friends, and Elephant and all *his* friends, so that the crowd round the Muula Tree was even greater than on the previous day, and Jackal and the Rabbit again could get no fruit.

"I say, you might make room for us!" Nkhandwe called out. "After all, it is my tree. I found it!" But no one took the slightest notice, and after a while Jackal and Kalulu went sadly away and sat underneath a Thorn Tree some distance off.

"What's the matter with you two?" demanded a voice from above. "You look about as cheerful as a pair of Crocodiles with toothache!"

"Hullo!" said Kalulu, looking up. "Is that you, Osprey?"

"It is. Is there anything I can do for you?"

"Maybe. I think I am getting an idea. Come down from your perch up there and I will tell you about it."

"Very well," answered Osprey, and fluttered down to the ground.

As quickly as he could, Kalulu told him about the Muula Tree and then he explained his idea. After that Nkhandwe, Kalulu and Osprey talked for a long time in eager whispers and, when they eventually parted company, all three were grinning happily.

Next morning, at an hour before dawn, Nkhandwe and Kalulu again went to the Muula Tree and found all the other animals already feeding on the fruit that had fallen during the night.

"My friends!" Kalulu called out in his loudest voice. "Stop eating for a moment while we ask whose land this is and to whom this tree belongs. It is not right to eat until we know. Let us ask Mlungu, the Great Spirit, and hear what He has to say!"

For a moment all the animals were silent, then Kudu spoke.

"You are right, Kalulu. Let us indeed ask whose tree this is." And the other animals agreed.

Kalulu, the Rabbit, looked upwards and lifted up his voice.

"O Mlungu, tell us whose land this is and to whom this Tree belongs?"

In silence they waited for an answer, but no answer came.

"Your voice is not loud enough, Kalulu," said Elephant at last. "I, myself, will ask the Great One!" Njobvu lifted up his trunk, trumpeted three times and roared: "O Mlungu, tell us whose land this is and to whom this Tree belongs?"

From far above them came the answer: "The land and the Tree belong to Jackal".

"What was that?" said Kudu.

"Whose is it?" asked Hartebeest.

"How can that be?" demanded Gnu, and all the animals began to chatter amongst themselves.

"SILENCE!" roared Elephant. "Silence, you foolish creatures, and I will ask again."

"O Mlungu," he bellowed once more. "Tell us to whom this Tree belongs?"

"To Jackal," said the distant Voice again.

"How can it belong to Jackal?" cried all the animals together.

"It does belong to Jackal. The land and the Tree are his and you shall eat no more of the fruit. Only Jackal is to eat it."

The animals looked at one another, then slowly turned away from the tree and moved off, shaking their heads in a puzzled way and grumbling a little as they went.

When they had all disappeared, Kalulu and Nkhandwe sat down under the tree and began to laugh. Presently
Osprey flew out of the topmost branch and came and
joined them and the three friends laughed and laughed
until their sides began to ache.

"You were superb, Osprey!" said the Rabbit. "Never
have I heard anything so impressive as your voice."

" 'Your voice isn't loud enough, Kalulu'," Nkhandwe
mimicked the Elephant. "What a good opinion Njobvu
has of himself! If only he'd known how funny he was!"

"What about our breakfast?" asked Nkhandwe at last.
"Have some of my fruit?"

"I wonder if I shall like it," murmured Osprey,
selecting the largest he could see. "Ugh!" he exclaimed,
a second later, "it's horrible! How can you eat such
stuff? No more for me! I think I'll go and catch some
fish." And away he flew without even waiting to hear
the Jackal's words of gratitude.

Meanwhile Kalulu had taken a bite out of one of the
ripest fruits and was making a wry face.

Nkhandwe looked at him. "Don't you like it?" he
asked in great surprise.

Kalulu shook his head. "It's horrible! How can you
eat such stuff?"

"I think it is delicious," said Nkhandwe. "And evidently
the other animals did, or they wouldn't have eaten it so
greedily."

"There is something in that," agreed Kalulu. "But
they will never eat it again and nor shall I. Mlungu—or
should I say Osprey?—is right. You, Jackal, alone of all
the animals shall eat the Muula fruit. The Tree is yours
for all time."

13

THE KINDLY ANT-BEAR

"GOOD morning, Njiri," the Ant-bear called out as Warthog came trotting past her burrow. "You seem to be in a great hurry. Where are you off to?"

"'Morning, Nkaka," he answered affably. "I am going to see Njobvu, the Elephant. He asked me to pay him a visit to-day."

"Did he, indeed?" Ant-bear sounded thoughtful. "I wonder what he is up to. I don't trust Njobvu further than I can see him—not so far, in fact. You'd better keep your wits about you, Njiri, or he'll trick you in some way."

"Oh dear! Do you really think so?"

"It wouldn't surprise me if he did! Anyway, I advise you to be careful."

"Oh, I will, Nkaka, I will! How kind of you to warn me. I am glad I came by this path. Are you staying here long?"

"I don't quite know," replied the Ant-bear. "I have so many burrows that I never stay long in one place. But

I expect I shall be here for a few days. Come and see me any time you like." Ant-bear was fond of the Warthog and she felt sorry for him. He was so ugly and so foolish, but he had a heart of gold and was always so charmingly grateful for any little kindness. She watched him trot away with an anxious look in her eyes and hoped that, for once, Njobvu, the Elephant, was being pleasant and friendly instead of cunning and dishonest, as so often was the case.

When Njiri reached the Elephant's favourite patch of scrub, he found that Njobvu was still breakfasting off the tree-tops, so he nosed out a root for himself and settled down to eat it.

"That's right!" Njobvu called out, graciously waving his trunk in the Warthog's direction. "Help yourself, Njiri! Make yourself at home. I shall have finished in a few minutes."

In those days it was the Warthog who had enormous ivory tusks while Elephant had only a small pair, and this made Njobvu very envious. Njiri's tusks were so huge that they trailed along the ground and, although Warthog would never admit it, they were a bit of a nuisance at times, and they weighed so much that he could not travel as fast as he would like. Still, he was tremendously proud of them and would not have parted with them for anything in the world. So he was delighted when Njobvu, having finished his breakfast, came over to him and said in a voice full of admiration, "What wonderful tusks you have, Njiri. I do believe they are the finest tusks in all Africa."

"Oh, do you think so?" Warthog almost blushed with pleasure. "How kind of you to say so! Your own tusks are very fine, of course, but I really do think mine are a little longer!"

"Far longer. Far bigger. Far more handsome altogether," agreed the Elephant. "I wonder if . . . but no, I could not ask you that." Njobvu sighed.

"What is it that you want to know?" Njiri had already forgotten the Ant-bear's warning and was thinking how kind and delightful the Elephant was.

"I really don't think I should . . . " Njobvu began. "No, I'm sure I ought not to ask . . . but . . . er . . . I was wondering if you would lend me your beautiful tusks for a day or two? I'd take the greatest care of them, of course, and you could have mine in the meantime if you liked. . . ." Njobvu paused hopefully and waited for Warthog's answer. It came almost at once.

"Why, certainly! I am sure you will look after them and I shall be very glad to have yours in exchange." And then and there Warthog unfastened his tusks and gave them to the Elephant, who hurriedly removed his own and put the big ones in their place. There was no doubt that Njiri's tusks suited the Elephant very well and he could not help wondering if they looked as handsome on himself. He hoped he would not look foolish in Elephant's little tusks. Carefully he tried them on, and as he did so it began to rain.

"Dear me, what a nuisance this rain is!" exclaimed Njobvu. "There is so little shelter here!"

"There isn't much," agreed Njiri. "It is on occasions like this that I envy Nkaka, the Ant-bear."

"Yes. It must be nice to live in a burrow," sighed the Elephant. "I can think of nothing I should like so much. But you and I will never live in burrows, for we cannot dig. Ah, well, I must be moving along. Thank you so much for coming to see me and for your lovely tusks."

"Thank *you*," replied Njiri politely. "You will bring them back in a day or two?" he added. There was just a shade of anxiety in his voice.

"Of course I will. Don't you start worrying. Your tusks will be all right!" With a farewell wave of his trunk, Njobvu moved off noiselessly through the scrub. Warthog watched him for a minute then, grunting gently

to himself, he turned and trotted back by the way that
he had come.

Three days passed without any sign of the Elephant,
and Njiri began to want his own tusks back again. On
the fourth day Njiri wondered if he should go and ask
Njobvu for them. On the fifth day Njiri decided that he
would have to go and ask Njobvu to give them back to
him. On the sixth day Njiri asked Njobvu to give them
back and was answered by a scornful laugh.

"You foolish Warthog!" said the Elephant with a sneer. "These tusks are far too good for you. Besides, you yourself, gave them to me!"

"Oh!" spluttered Njiri, almost choking with indignation. "That isn't true. How wicked you are! You know I only *lent* them to you and you said you'd bring them back in a day or two."

"And you thought I meant it? How stupid you are! I've always wanted these tusks and now I've got them and I am going to keep them. You are never going to have them again. They are mine, now. Mine! MINE!" Njobvu gave a heartless laugh, then, trumpeting victoriously, he swung round and made off as fast as he could.

It was a very dejected Warthog that passed the Ant-bear's burrow later in the day. Nkaka saw at once that something was wrong and hurriedly called out: "What is the matter, Njiri? Come and tell me what has happened."

Warthog stopped and turned a woebegone face towards the Ant-bear.

"Dear, kind Nkaka," he said sadly. "Elephant is right and I am indeed a foolish Warthog. I forgot your warning and now Njobvu has tricked me out of my beautiful tusks and has left me his little ones instead." Dolefully, Njiri told the whole story.

Nkaka became more and more indignant as she listened.

"Poor Njiri!" she said. "It is a shame, and Njobvu shall be punished for it! He shall never have a real home, and he shall be hunted for all time for the sake of his ivory tusks. But you, Warthog, shall be safe, and you shall live in a burrow for the rest of your days."

"But how can I do that, Nkaka?" Warthog asked incredulously. "You know I cannot dig!"

"I know, Njiri. But you shall use my burrows—I have so many and am always making new ones. There are more than enough for us both."

"How can I ever thank you!" The happy Warthog could scarcely believe his good fortune. "I have always longed to live in a burrow and now you make it possible for me to do so. Dear Ant-bear! Kind Ant-bear! I will call down a blessing on you. May you never have to seek for food. Even while you are lying down, your food shall come to you, and may nothing ever break our friendship!"

*　　*　　*　　*　　*

Nothing has broken it. Generations of Warthogs have lived in the burrows of the Ant-bears, and always they have remained the best of friends. And the Ant-bear does not have to seek for food. All she has to do when she feels hungry is to put out her long sticky tongue and wait for insects to alight upon it. Bad luck on the insects, perhaps, but it is all the Elephant's fault!

14

THE BRAGGING BAT

In the middle of Africa, on top of an ant-hill, there grew a hollow tree and in that tree lived Mleme, the first of all the Bats. He was a most conceited creature and prided himself greatly on his bravery, and his manner towards the other animals was so condescending that they all agreed that he was quite insufferable.

"Even if it is wrong and wicked," said Nantusi, the Toad, to Changa, the Lemur, "I can't help wishing that something would give Mleme a really bad fright. It would do him good! Only last night he made himself most objectionable to me."

"He did?" Changa immediately looked interested. "What happened?"

"It was very distressing! I'd had the misfortune to meet a snake and I was just puffing myself out so that it could not swallow me, when along comes Mleme and what does he do? He bursts out laughing! 'Goodness,' he says, 'you do look a sight, Nantusi! Whyever are you blowing yourself out like that?' So rude! And what was I to do? There was the snake, and there was I only half puffed up and so angry that I had no breath left to puff with! Luckily, Mongoose happened to come along at that moment and the snake hurriedly moved off, otherwise who knows what might not have occurred! And all the time Mleme sat on the branch of a tree, laughing as if he'd never stop. 'Fancy being frightened of a snake!' he calls out. 'You'd have been frightened if you had been me!' says I. 'Not I!' answers Mleme. 'I'm afraid of nothing!' says he, and he starts laughing again."

"What a shame!" exclaimed the Lemur. "But how typical of him! Mleme is always bragging about his courage and not being frightened of anything. He'd be a much nicer creature if he was not so conceited and unkind! Yes, I do wish we could give him a fright. It would serve him right and be very good for him, too!"

"Let us go to Kalulu, the Rabbit," Nantusi suggested. "He is so clever and full of ideas. He will think of a way in which to frighten that Bat."

Kalulu, the Rabbit, was at home resting after a busy day. He was delighted to see Toad and Lemur and listened most attentively to their story.

"I quite agree," he said, when Toad had finished

speaking. "Something should certainly be done about it!" and for some minutes he puffed thoughtfully at his pipe. "How would it be if we were to ask Njobvu, the Elephant, to knock down the hollow tree in which Mleme lives?" Kalulu suggested at last. "That ought to give him a shock—especially if we make sure that he is at home when it happens!"

"What a splendid idea!" said Nantusi, the Toad.

"The very thing!" exclaimed the Lemur. "How clever you are, Kalulu!"

"And will you take the message to Njobvu?" asked the Toad.

"No, Nantusi. Elephant is no friend of mine and I have no wish to see him. But there is no reason why you should not go and ask him."

"Oh!" said Toad unhappily. Nantusi was a little afraid of Njobvu—he was so big, so grand, and generally so crushing to any of the smaller animals who dared to approach him. Then he remembered that it was in a Good Cause that he would be asking for the Elephant's help, so he cheered up and agreed to take the message.

Elephant was enjoying his morning bath when Nantusi found him the next day, so Toad sat down on the river-bank and waited patiently for him to finish. Njobvu took a very long time about it, but at length he emerged from the water and Toad went to meet him.

"I bring a message, Njobvu," began Nantusi, speaking rather nervously. "We want your help. . . ."

"Run away, little Toad, and do not bother me." The Elephant looked disdainfully down his trunk and walked on.

Nantusi hopped after him, feeling still more nervous but a little bit indignant.

"It is nothing difficult, Njobvu," he said. "We only want you to knock down Mleme's hollow tree."

"Go away quickly, little Toad, and do not annoy me, or I will stamp upon you!" Elephant quickened his pace, but Nantusi was now so indignant that he forgot to be nervous and once more hopped after him.

"Njobvu!" he began again. "Surely you . . ."

"Go away!" roared the Elephant, and stamped his foot. Nantusi gave one jump, turned and fled back to his friends, his little heart palpitating with anger as much as with fright.

Kalulu, the Rabbit, and Changa, the Lemur, were angry, too, as well as disappointed, when they heard how Njobvu had treated the poor Toad. "How hateful of Njobvu!" said Kalulu, and "He's abominable!" said Changa, which made them both feel a little better. There was nothing for it, however, but to try and think of some other plan for dealing with Mleme, and all three animals sat down and racked their brains for a Really Good Idea.

Suddenly Kalulu looked up and sniffed the air. It was very still and scarcely a rustle sounded in the long grass. Far away the sky looked black and threatening and a distant rumble echoed in the hills.

"Thunder!" muttered Kalulu. "If I am not mistaken there's a tremendous storm brewing. We'd better all get back to our homes while we can!"

Nantusi and Changa scrambled to their feet and hurried off. There had been no thunder for a long time but they could remember dimly how terrifying a bad storm could be. Other animals had also heard that distant rumble and the path that led past Mleme's hollow tree was alive with scuttling forms.

It was this unusual activity that wakened Mleme and, after blinking his beady little eyes for a minute, he peered out to see what was happening.

"Hullo! What's up and where are you off to in such a hurry?" he asked the Bushbuck as he dashed past.

"Storm coming!" answered Bushbuck shortly.

"Well, what of it?" demanded Mleme. "Who's afraid of a storm?"

"All sensible creatures, you foolish Bat!" came the answer.

"*I'm* not! I'm afraid of nothing!" bragged Mleme, and he began to laugh and to jeer at all the animals as they came by. Then he broke into a little song

> "Bushbuck is a coward,
> But I am very brave
> (tra-la-la, tra-la).
> Toad, he is a coward,
> Lemur is a coward,
> All of you are cowards
> And only I am brave.
>   Tra-la-la."

Again Mleme laughed, then he started on a second verse:

> "Although the Elephant is large,
> He isn't brave like me.
>   Tra-la . . ."

A flash of lightning forked the sky and the "tra-la-la" died in Mleme's throat as a terrific clap of thunder rent the air. The song came to an abrupt end and Mleme swallowed twice. Never before had he known such thunder and, for the first time in his life, he did not feel at all brave.

A second flash of lightning was followed by an even louder clap of thunder and Mleme began to squeak with fright and, when a third flash came, splitting the hollow tree from top to bottom, he flew out in a panic, screeching and chattering, and so dazed with fear that he clung upside down to the nearest branch and hid his face with his wings.

Rain began to fall and gradually the thunder grew more distant, but still Mleme clung to his tree, hanging head downwards and not daring to show his face. Bye and bye the storm cleared and Toad and Lemur came

along the path again. As they neared Mleme's hollow
tree, they saw Njobvu, the Elephant, in the distance. At
the same moment they saw the blasted tree.

"Look!" squeaked Changa, his voice shrill with excitement. "Look at Mleme's tree! Do you think Njobvu
decided to help us after all?"

"Not he!" said Toad. "Elephant never did that! The
storm has helped us and helped us far more effectively
than Njobvu could have done. I wonder where Mleme
is?"

They looked around and at length they found him—a
very subdued and humble Bat, who seemed overjoyed

to see them and was touchingly grateful when they offered to help him look for a new home.

They were on the point of setting out on their search when Njobvu came by.

"Ah!" said he, on seeing Nantusi. "The little Toad! What was that you were saying this morning about wanting my help? If I agree to help you, what will you give me?"

"Nothing, Njobvu!" Toad answered sweetly. "We find we don't need your help at all!"

He bowed politely and, calling to Changa and Mleme to follow him, Nantusi hopped away, leaving the Elephant speechless with surprise.

Since that day, Mleme has been a changed character, but he and all his descendants have always slept hanging upside down, with their wings folded over their faces and their ears, so that if a storm comes they are, at least, unable either to see or hear it.

15

THE FAMINE AND THE
FRUIT TREE

"THE question is," said Njobvu, the Elephant, "is it good to eat? Also, what is its name? That's important, too."

There was no answer, for none of the animals knew. They just continued to sit in a circle, gazing hungrily at the tree and wondering if its luscious fruits were poisonous or not. The matter was urgent because there was a famine in the land. Everything was parched and dry and much of the country had been swept by bush-fires, so that there were no young tender shoots upon the trees, no succulent green grass upon the plain. In all the land

there seemed to be nothing save the fruit of this one tree, and no one knew if it was safe to eat it.

"Why doesn't someone try it and see?" suggested Nchefu, the Eland. "Then we should soon know!"

"Fine!" said Bushbuck. "Why don't you try it yourself, Nchefu?"

"Oh, I'm not hungry and I don't really care for fruit." Eland was in a great hurry with his reply.

"How would it be," began Kalulu slowly, "if we were to send a messenger to the Wise-Old-Python-who-lives-in-the-middle-of-the-Lake? He is sure to know the name and whether it is good to eat."

"Yes, yes!" cried all the animals together. "The Wise-Old-Python is sure to know! Let us send a messenger at once!"

"Send Bushbuck. Bushbuck is the fastest of us all!" Eland smiled maliciously and a chorus of agreement came from all the other animals.

"I don't mind going," said Bushbuck, "though goodness knows how I'm to get across the Lake. But I'll manage somehow. Good-bye! I'll be back as soon as I can!" and away he galloped amidst cries of "Good-bye!", "Good luck!" and "Good old Bushbuck!"

The sun was high in the heavens when Bushbuck returned, tired and thirsty, on the following day. Immediately the animals crowded round him, each one asking a different question.

"What's the name?" said one. "Is it poisonous?" demanded another. "Can we eat it?" said a third. "What did Python say?" asked a fourth.

"The name," panted Bushbuck, "is . . . the name is . . ." He paused with a bewildered look on his face. "I can't remember!" he said in an awful whisper. "I can't remember anything about it—not even if Python said that we could eat it!"

"I don't suppose you ever saw Python at all!" exclaimed Eland nastily. "Otherwise I don't see how you could have forgotten. Forgotten, indeed!"

"I did see Python!" Bushbuck retorted angrily. "I know I saw him. I can remember what he looked like. Magnificent and so wise! But I can't remember what he said. I crossed the Lake on a strip of bark and I ate some grass that grew by the shore—delicious grass—and then I think I must have gone to sleep . . ."

"You went to sleep?" thundered the Elephant in a voice of fury. "You went to sleep?"

"Yes! I felt tired. I only slept for a little while. One can't go on for ever without sleep!"

"Nonsense! Disgraceful!" snorted Njobvu. "I consider that you have been foolish, careless and lazy, therefore I shall spank you."

"But we must send another messenger!" cried Eland. "We *must* know if we can eat the fruit of this tree."

"Certainly, Nchefu," agreed the Elephant. "You shall go yourself since you are so anxious about it!"

"Oh!" Nchefu looked as if he wished he hadn't spoken in such a hurry. "Don't you think it would be better to send Hartebeest? Hartebeest runs more swiftly than I do."

"No, Nchefu, you can go yourself!"

So, with a very bad grace, the Eland went.

He returned at sundown on the following day. With joyful cries, the hungry animals all gathered round to hear his news.

"What is the name?" they asked. And, "Is it good? Can we eat it?"

"The name," answered Eland, "is . . ." Then *he* paused with a bewildered look upon his face.

"Hurry up, Nchefu!" exclaimed Hartebeest. "Tell us quickly."

But Nchefu couldn't tell them quickly for, like Bushbuck, he had forgotten everything the Python had said. And when the animals heard that he, too, had eaten some of the grass that grew beside the Lake and had fallen asleep, they were very angry indeed and were all agreed that he deserved to be spanked. So spanked Nchefu was—extremely hard—until he wished he'd never even seen the grass that grew by the still blue waters of the Lake.

The next messenger to be sent was Hartebeest, and everything happened to him exactly as it had to Bush-buck and to Eland, and *he* got spanked and so did all the other animals, for they all forgot what Python had told them. All except Kamba, the Tortoise. He had not been sent as a messenger, and every time he offered to go the others all laughed at him and said rude things.

"We'll all be dead before you reach the Lake, old Slow-coach!" was Eland's unkind comment.

"Silly little Kamba! There won't be any fruit left by the time you get back!" was Hartebeest's remark.

At length, however, when one animal after another had failed in his mission and all of them were as hungry as hungry, because they had been living on water and nothing else for a whole week, Tortoise again suggested that he should go and ask the Python about the Fruit Tree.

"Don't be silly!" began Hartebeest again.

"What's the good?" asked Bushbuck wearily.

"Why shouldn't he go if he wants to?" demanded Kudu. "*We* are no worse off if he does!"

"That's true!" said Nchefu, the Eland. "Besides, we've all been spanked, so why shouldn't Kamba be spanked?"

"Very well," agreed the Elephant. "Kamba shall go, and if he fails we'll all spank him in turn!"

So Kamba set off, and his wife went with him for a little way because she wanted to give him some advice.

"Now don't you be tempted to eat anything on the way—either there or back," she said. "*I* think there is something peculiar about that grass that grows beside the Lake. And mind you are polite to everyone you meet."

"Very well, my dear," said Kamba and, with a fare-well smile, he hurried onwards, while his wife returned home.

It took Tortoise three days to reach the Lake, and when he got there he could see no signs of the strip of bark on which the others had crossed to Python's Island. Kamba was almost in despair when he saw a family of Crocodiles coming towards him. There were six of them—Crocodile and his wife and four extremely plain daughters. Tortoise thought he had never seen such ugly children before, but as soon as they came close, he bowed politely and said "good morning!"

"Good morning," replied the Crocodiles, and the Crocodile's wife smiled what she thought was a gracious smile and said:

"I don't think you have seen my dear little children before? Are they not beautiful?"

"Yes, indeed, Madam," answered Kamba with a gulp. What else could he say? He had to be polite!

"I am so glad you admire them," she gushed.

"And what, may I ask, are you doing in these parts?" asked the Crocodile quickly, for he always felt embarrassed when his wife began to talk about the children.

"I have an important question to ask the Wise-Old-Python, but I don't know how to get to his island, as I have no raft or canoe."

"My dear fellow!" exclaimed the Crocodile. "Let me take you there. If you just sit on my back, I can ferry you across in no time."

"Oh, that would be kind!" Tortoise was delighted. Without waiting another minute, he clambered on to the Crocodile's back and was carried over to the island.

The Python greeted him with a smile and looked wiser than ever when Kamba told him what had happened and apologised for troubling him yet again over the matter of the Fruit Tree.

"Foolish creatures!" murmured the Python. "And many of them so rude and mannerless! But you, Kamba, have done well so far. See that you are wise on your journey back. The tree to which you refer is the Munjubele and the fruit is very good to eat."

"Munjubele, Munjubele," muttered Tortoise, over and

over again. Then he thanked the Python for being so kind and helpful and bade him farewell.

Crocodile had waited for him, so that in next to no time at all Kamba was back on the Lake shore and saying good-bye to the Crocodiles.

"Munjubele," he began, "I mean . . . er . . . I cannot say how grateful I am . . . (Munjubele) . . . I really don't know what I should have done without you. So many thanks. Munjubele." And muttering "Munjubele, Munjubele" to himself, Tortoise crawled along the path that led away from the Lake.

He had not gone far when he noticed some beautiful green grass growing close by. He did not remember seeing it on his way down, so no doubt he had been looking in the wrong direction, otherwise he felt sure he could not have passed by without eating just a little. It was so green, so luscious, so tempting. And he was so very hungry. A good meal was just what he needed now to fortify him for the journey back!

Kamba was about to take a mouthful when a small snake slithered out of the clump of grass and nearly bumped into him.

"I beg your pardon!" Kamba backed a little. "I am afraid I got in your way. Is this *your* grass? I wonder if you would mind if I ate a little? I'm very hungry and have a long way to go."

"I don't mind at all," answered the snake. "But I don't advise you to eat it. It tastes all right but has a queer effect on the memory. Still, if you are *very* hungry . . ."

"No, no," said Tortoise hurriedly. "Thank you so much for telling me. For a moment I had forgotten that I'd been told not to eat anything. Munjubele! That was a narrow squeak!" he murmured as he crawled away. "If I'd eaten that I suppose I would have forgotten all about the Munjubele! Whew! I *am* glad I didn't."

Three days later, just as the sun was setting and all the animals were walking wearily down to the water-hole, they noticed a small something lying in the middle of the path. Bushbuck and Kudu hastened their steps a little and went forward to investigate and, to their amazement, found it was a Tortoise—a thin, dusty, exhausted Tortoise who had fainted from hunger by the way.

Quickly they went and got some water and splashed it over him. Then they waited expectantly for him to revive. Five minutes passed before they saw any signs of movement. Then a tired little voice began to chant:

> "It's name is Munjubele,
> And it's very good to eat."

Again and again Kamba mumbled these words, at first so faintly that no one could catch their meaning. Gradually the voice grew stronger and the animals heard, and knew that Tortoise—gallant little Tortoise— had succeeded in his mission and had saved them.

They carried him carefully to the Munjubele Tree and laid him down beside it. Then they collected a heap of the very choicest fruit for him and sent for Kamba's wife. And *then* they fell upon the fruit themselves and ate and ate and ate till they could eat no more and, when the moon rose, golden-red, from behind the purple mountains, it shone upon a happy circle of well-fed animals and an even happier pair of Tortoises.

16

THE BARREL OF WATER

NYALUGWE, the Leopard, crouched upon the lowest branch of a Mahogany tree and gazed at his reflection in the pool below. There was something wrong with the third whisker on the left-paw side. It would *not* lie quite right and this displeased him greatly. Nyalugwe was very particular about his appearance and spent more time admiring himself than any other animal in the forest. In consequence, he was generally considered to be the smartest of them all. And, of course, if you are as smart as all that, you have to be careful about the set of your third whisker on the left-paw side—or, indeed, of

any whisker! So Nyalugwe was annoyed, and in his
annoyance he forgot all about Fisi, the Hyæna, who was
waiting patiently to see him when he had finished his
toilet.

Minutes passed while Nyalugwe frowned at his reflection, and it was only when the Hyæna gave a deferential
cough that the Leopard suddenly remembered. What, he
wondered, did Fisi want? It was unusual for the Hyæna
to call upon him, so possibly it was something interesting
. . . and it really wasn't any good bothering about that
whisker! Nyalugwe got up and stretched himself. Then
he climbed gracefully to the ground.

"Well, what is it?" he asked, as Fisi trotted forward.

"News!" said the Hyæna. "Gorilla has found a barrel
of water—a mysterious barrel—and he is offering a prize
to the first person who can drink it all in one day."

"Oh? That sounds easy enough! Is that all there is to
it?"

"That is all."

"H'm!" Nyalugwe looked thoughtful for a minute.
"Where did Gorilla find this barrel of water?" he asked
at length.

"No one knows," replied the Hyæna. "Some say it was
washed up by the sea."

"Indeed? Then I think I will go and see if I can find
out more about it. It was very sensible of you to come
and tell me. I am much obliged."

"A pleasure, I assure you!" Fisi smirked with delight,
murmured "good-day" and trotted off along the river-
bank in search of Mvu, the Hippopotamus.

Nyalugwe also stalked off. He travelled for several
hours in a north-easterly direction until he reached a
large clearing in the middle of the forest. Here it was
evident that something unusual was about to happen,
for almost all the animals of the jungle were gathered
there and others were still arriving. At one end of the
clearing sat a huge Gorilla, beside him, his charming

daughter. In the centre stood a barrel and it was at this that everyone was looking.

For a moment Nyalugwe surveyed the scene in dignified silence. Then he walked over to his friend the Lion and enquired if he knew anything about the mysterious barrel.

"Just an ordinary barrel of water, I believe," Mkango said. "To be drunk in one day, they say. Absurdly easy, of course! I could manage it in an hour."

"Ridiculously easy!" agreed the Leopard. "I reckon I could do it in fifty minutes. I shall win the prize!"

"You haven't won yet!" snorted the Lion. "Personally, I feel sure that I shall win. When I said 'an hour', I was just speaking figuratively. I could do it in half an hour—or even less!"

"And what would be the good of that?" demanded Mvu, the Hippopotamus, who had that moment arrived. "I should beat you easily. After all, what is a barrel of water to me? A mere mouthful! I should scarcely notice it."

The argument was getting quite heated when suddenly a voice called for silence in the clearing and the terms of the competition were explained. As Fisi and Mkango had said, the barrel of water had to be drunk in one day and the first person to succeed would be the winner. Lots were to be cast for the order of starting. There was a good deal of excitement over this, and Mvu, the Hippopotamus, was delighted when he found that he had drawn the shortest straw and that he would therefore have the first chance. Feeling a little self-conscious, he approached the barrel and took a deep breath. . . .

A moment later the silence in the clearing was shattered by a sudden roar and the startled onlookers all watched with amazement as they saw Mvu leap wildly into the air. He stood upon his hind legs and he stood upon his front legs, and he roared and he bellowed and he howled. Then, with tears streaming from his little pig-like eyes,

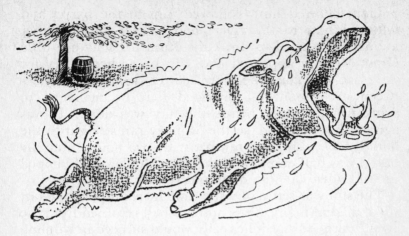

he rushed away to the river and frantically washed out his mouth. For the water in the barrel had burnt him and stung him and never before had Mvu known anything like it. Which was not surprising because although the water looked like water, it was nothing of the sort. It was Rum—good, strong ship's Rum, washed up by the tide with other wreckage after a great storm at sea.

The animals could not understand what had happened and there was a good deal of speculation and much laughter over Mvu's evident discomfiture. Nyalugwe was particularly pleased, as he had thought that the Hippopotamus was indeed a competitor to be feared. Now he felt more confident than ever that he would win the prize.

Silence again fell on the clearing as he approached the barrel and all eyes were fixed on him as he placed his paws upon it, took a deep breath and gulped down a mouthful of the "water". There was an instant's pause then, howling at the top of his voice, Nyalugwe began to dance. He danced upon his hind legs and he danced upon his front legs and ran madly round in circles with his tongue hanging out like a piece of red flannel. Then he, too, rushed away to the river to wash out his mouth.

Lion followed him—followed him to the barrel and followed him to the river; and so did all the other animals who tried to drink the Rum. At length a little Grass Monkey appeared and said he wished to try for the prize. But could he, he asked, lie down and rest between each mouthful provided that he managed to drink up the water before the day was done? It was agreed that he could, so the Monkey ran straight to the barrel, took a sip, and ran back. In two hours' time the barrel was half empty and the little Monkey had popped up and down one hundred and twenty times.

The sun was setting by the time he ran up for the last sip of all and many of the animals had returned from the river in order to see if he really would succeed in winning through. Nyalugwe was back and, so that he might get a better view, had climbed a nearby tree. He was still feeling a little dazed and simply could not understand how the little Monkey had managed to drink so much of the dreadful fire-water—even in sips. Absently he stared at the long grass from which the Monkey had come . . . was it a trick of the light or was something moving down there? Nyalugwe peered down intently. Yes, something *was* moving—several things were moving —several Monkeys! Hundreds of Monkeys! Little Grass Monkeys—all exactly alike!

At that moment a burst of applause announced that the barrel of water was at last empty and that the Grass Monkey had won. In the excitement that followed no one noticed that Nyalugwe had left his tree—no one—not even the little Monkeys—until a sudden snarl of fury revealed his presence in their midst.

"Cheats! Frauds! Tricksters!" roared Nyalugwe, bristling with rage and striking wildly at the nearest Monkey. "How dare you try and deceive us all. You shall be punished for this!" Leopard made a grab at another Monkey's tail.

Shrieking and chattering with terror, the little Monkeys

turned and ran, while all the animals crowded round asking each other what had happened. No sooner did they hear than they, too, joined in the chase, and they harried those Monkeys and chivvied those Monkeys, till the Monkeys left the grass and took to the trees. Then all the animals who could climb followed them into the trees and chased them to the very tippest tops of them, and there the Monkeys stayed—because no one else could climb so high. And to this day that is where the little Monkeys live, hardly ever daring to come down to the ground in case their deceitfulness has not been forgotten.

TORTOISE TRIUMPHANT

"I FAIL to see," remarked Kamba, the Tortoise, to his wife, "why Njobvu, the Elephant, should give himself such airs—just because he happens to be bigger than anyone else. What does size matter? And Mvu, the Hippopotamus, is almost as bad."

"Ill-mannered and conceited—that's what they are!" Tortoise's wife gave a contemptuous sniff.

"I suppose it is because they are stronger than the rest of us," mused Kamba.

"What if they are? What's the good of strength if you haven't got a brain, I'd like to know?"

"Haven't they got brains?" asked Kamba in surprise. He was a humble character and always thought everyone else was cleverer than himself.

"Not what *I* call brain," replied the Tortoise's wife loftily. "Now, listen to me, Kamba," she continued. "I have got a plan for teaching both Njobvu and Mvu a lesson and, if I am not much mistaken, it won't be long before they will be only too pleased to treat you as an equal!"

"Oh?" Tortoise immediately looked interested. "What is this plan?"

Kamba's wife told him. And, as he listened, Kamba's smile gradually became a grin, and the grin spread and spread until it seemed to go three times round his funny little face.

"Oh, excellent!" he chuckled. "Magnificent! A truly splendid idea! I'll go at once and challenge them." Chortling with delight, Kamba set off to pay a call on Mvu, the Hippopotamus.

Mvu was blowing bubbles in the middle of the river, with only his ears and his little pig-like eyes showing above the water, and Tortoise had to shout at him several times before he paid the slightest attention. At length he rose slowly to the surface, stared haughtily at Kamba and told him not to come making a noise on *his* river-bank.

"And since when," demanded Kamba boldly, "has the bank belonged to you?"

"How dare you speak to me like that!" Mvu spluttered with rage. "You miserable little object! You impudent reptile! Go away at once!"

"Why should I, if I don't want to? I suppose you think you are stronger than I am, just because you are a little bigger?"

"Of course I'm stronger than you!"

"I very much doubt it,'" said Kamba. "It is all very well to brag like that, but you wouldn't dare to take me on at a tug-of-war!"

"What?" roared the Hippopotamus. "Not take you on? You must be mad! Why, I'd pull you over quicker than a Snake can bite!"

"Not you!" replied the Tortoise. "I'm stronger than I look. Though, mind you, I don't say that *I* could pull you across . . ."

"I should think not!"

"Well, will you take me on at sunrise to-morrow? And if neither of us pulls the other over, we'll pull until the vine-rope breaks and then we shall know that we are equally strong."

"I certainly will," said Mvu, the Hippopotamus. "And when I've pulled you across . . ."

" 'Quicker than a Snake can bite,' " murmured Kamba impertinently.

" . . . I'll pull you out of your shell and spank you so hard that you'll wish you had never been born."

"So you may think!" said Kamba cheerfully, "but we shall see!" And, without more ado, he crawled away to seek out Njobvu, the Elephant.

Njobvu was having forty winks under the shade of a Boabab tree and he was extremely angry at being woken up by Tortoise. And when Kamba suggested that he was no stronger than himself, the Elephant trumpeted with rage and tore up a tree by its roots, just to show how strong he was.

Putting his head on one side, Kamba looked at the unfortunate sapling.

"Pretty fair!" he said, critically. "Of course, that's only a very young tree!"

"Oh, it is, is it?" bellowed Njobvu furiously. "Well, what about this?" He promptly rooted up another, much larger tree.

"So-so!" said Tortoise airily. "Not at all bad, in fact. However, I don't suppose you would care to take *me* on at a tug-of-war?"

"Ha, ha, ha!" The Elephant roared with laughter. "That's the best joke I've heard for a long time! You must be mad, Kamba! Why, I'd pull you over quicker than a Bee can sting!"

"Will you take me on at sunrise to-morrow?"

"Certainly I will," replied the Elephant. "And when I've pulled you across . . ."

" 'Quicker than a Bee can sting,' " murmured the Tortoise.

" . . . I'll toss you up into the air until you are so giddy that you'll wish you'd never heard of a tug-of-war. And then I'll spank you!"

"Well, we shall see," said Kamba coolly. "If neither of us succeeds in pulling the other over, we will pull until the vine-rope breaks. Then we will know that we are equally strong. Do you agree?"

"Oh, yes, I agree! But you are going to be sorry for your impertinence. I wouldn't be you for much!"

"And I wouldn't be you for anything!" returned Kamba stoutly, and he crawled away to report to his wife.

That night was spent by Mvu, who was as conscientious as he was conceited, in doing exercises and seeing that his muscles were well oiled. He ate the lightest of dinners, for he believed in going into strict training, even for an affair of this sort. Njobvu, on the other hand, was quite satisfied that he was by far the strongest animal in the whole countryside and so had just as large a dinner as usual and made no effort to train.

Tortoise spent the night looking for a long, strong vine-rope.

At dawn he found it—the longest, strongest rope he had ever seen, and he hurried off as fast as he could to give one end to the Elephant and the other to the Hippopotamus. And because of the length of the rope and height of the grass, neither animal could see the other end and both, of course, thought that Kamba, the Tortoise, was there. But Kamba was somewhere in between, and when he shouted: "Are you ready? Go!" each animal braced himself and pulled on the rope for all he was worth, thinking that with one good tug it would all be over.

To their amazement, they could not make an inch of ground. Again Mvu braced himself, and again and again,

and he pulled till his well-oiled muscles bulged. But it made no difference.

"Phew!" he whistled to himself. "The strength of this Tortoise is simply *stu*-pendous!"

Meanwhile Njobvu, the Elephant, was pulling with all *his* might. Never in all his life had he pulled so hard, but not one fraction of an inch could he gain. And after awhile he said to himself:

"Phew! The strength of this Tortoise is simply *stu*-pendous!"

Hour after hour passed, and still the Elephant and the Hippopotamus pulled and tugged and neither would give way, although they both were beginning to tire. At last Tortoise decided they had had enough so, taking a sharp piece of stone, he carefully cut through the vine-rope, right in the very middle. Instantly there came a terrific splash from one end, and a tremendous crash at the other, for Mvu had been standing on the river-bank and, as the rope gave, he fell backwards into the water. And so great was the splash he made that for the next week he was kept busy replying to the complaints that were lodged by all the Crocodiles and Fishes who had been disturbed. Njobvu, in falling, had crashed against a tree, and so great was the impact that the whole tree fell to the ground. It took Elephant quite a while to sort himself out from the tangle of branches, earth and roots, and when he had done so, he found a smiling Tortoise looking up at him.

"I do hope you haven't hurt yourself?" Kamba asked. "That was a fine tug-of-war. I wonder the rope stood up to such a strain! Anyway, I am sure you will agree now that we are equally strong?"

"So it seems!" Njobvu sounded very disgruntled. "I still find it very hard to believe!" He walked away, slowly and painfully, shaking his head in a bewildered kind of way.

Kamba grinned and hurried along the river-bank.

"Are you all right?" he called out anxiously to Mvu.

"I must congratulate you on such a magnificent display of strength. We really do seem to be equal, don't we?"

Mvu, the Hippopotamus, was almost too dazed to speak, but he nodded his head in agreement.

"Perhaps you will come and dine with us one evening?" continued Kamba pleasantly. "My wife will be delighted to see you. We might ask Njobvu, the Elephant, to come too. He is about the only fellow in our class, isn't he?"

Again Mvu nodded and, with an effort, forced himself to speak.

"I am sure we should both be honoured," he said, and, closing his little eyes, he sank beneath the surface of the water.